Life is like a Box of Chocolates

Dana Zheteyeva

Copyright © 2022 Dana Zheteyeva.

All rights reserved. No part of this book may be reproduced in any form or by any electronic or mechanical means, including information storage and retrieval systems, without permission in writing from the author and publisher, except by reviewers, who may quote brief passages in a review.

ISBN: 978-1-958517-51-2   (Paperback Edition)
ISBN: 978-1-958517-50-5   (E-book Edition)

Some characters and events in this book are fictitious and products of the author's imagination. Any similarity to real persons, living or dead, is coincidental and not intended by the author.

Book Ordering Information

The Regency Publishers, International
7 Bell Yard London WO2A2JR

info@theregencypublishers.com
www.theregencypublishers.international
+44 20 8133 0466

Printed in the United States of America

Contents

"You never know what destiny will offer you…" 1
A Train Story 17
A Vision 31

"You never know what destiny will offer you..."

Since early years Diana's dream was to become a surgeon, just like her parents. She did an extra study at school in order to get into medical school later and was very curious, asking tons of questions from her parents. They also had a huge library with hundreds of medical books, which she loved to peruse.

When she first started talking about becoming a surgeon, she was only 8 years old. Her mum knew her hyperactive child and thought that it might be difficult for her to stay in one place and study so much. So, she said that a surgeon's hands must be so precise, firm, and at the same time gentle, that his hands could be only compared to a violinist's hands.

For Diana the decision was obvious and when the next school year was about to start, she told her parents that she wanted to go to the music school and learn how to play the violin.

Usually, parents brought their children to the local music school at the age of 4-5... Diana was 8, turning 9 in November, and she was a tall child. She was standing out in that group of newcomers. Besides, they were indeed little children, who were afraid or did not even understand what they were doing there. Diana, on the contrary, knew exactly why she was there.

The teachers of the admission committee were surprised and amused to see such a big child among the newbies. The entrance exam was to guess what keys one of the teachers was playing on the piano keys and repeat the melody that they played there too. Diana did that easily and was unwillingly accepted to her first grade. That was her first step on the long way of becoming a surgeon. She might not even remember that later, but it was that first step.

The music school was not fun at all, but she was a determined child. She had a goal and was moving towards it. She wanted to grow up sooner and become someone, who would bring some use to the people and this world.

So, when the summer before her last year of school began, she asked her parents to help her get a job at a hospital, as she wanted to try and see for herself what it was to work there. She was happy to do anything and anywhere, just to see with her own eyes how doctors saved lives day by day and make her humble contribution even by mopping the floors.

To tell the truth, her parents were not happy about her choice of profession. Being surgeons themselves during Soviet times and later in independent Kazakhstan, they knew the difference and they knew all the disadvantages of the job. Besides, they were people of principles and were treating people because they truly wanted to cure them, not because they wanted to earn more money on their patients.

Anyway, Diana did not know about their reasons, and they decided not to share them with her for now. So, for the summer job they offered her to work as a nurse's aide at the regional oncology treatment centre, where her father used to work as a surgeon. Everybody knew who she was, but she asked them to treat her as a usual aide – she would not accept a nepotistic attitude, she wanted to feel everything for herself.

The department that she was assigned to was on the top floor of that four-storied building. It was a thoracal department, a surgery block, and an Intensive Care Unit. She was still fifteen years old and legally she could not work at such places yet, so she asked the HR lady to add her one year on the papers and not tell that to anyone.

She had a medical uniform from her mother, so it was not a problem. She was washing and starching those white gowns of her parents and sometimes for her brother since she was twelve.

The first morning she arrived at work and introduced herself to the personnel. There were surgeons, nurses, nurse's aides, and a hospital matron.

The surgeons obviously knew her as they used to work with her parents. There was actually a period of Diana's life when they lived in one of the wings of the old oncological centre before they moved into their new apartment. So, those doctors, much younger then, remembered the little boisterous girl. Now Diana wanted to prove that she was all grown-up and serious.

Her duties were to wash the floors in all the wards, ICU, corridors, toilets, and staircases. Besides the floors, she needed to wipe every bed, bedside tables, all windowsills, doors, handles, etc. with a 3% chlorine solution. Also, she needed to clean the medical procedure unit and the dressing ward every other hour and then switch on the UV sterilization there. One of the duties was to bring food for the patients on their floor from the dining room, which was on the ground floor. She was doing that with another aide girl of course. And they used a trolley and a lift for that. Twice a week in the afternoon, there was a delivery of medical stuff and each department usually sent someone to the storage room to get the necessary number of saline solutions, glucose, plasm, the blood of different types, syringes, disposable operation gowns, I.V. fluid giving sets, etc. One would be a nurse so that she could get the right stuff for her department.

It was 1992, medicine was free for the patients, even the most severe oncological cases were treated for free. Face masks were different from what we are used to wearing nowadays. Every medical worker made his own face mask from the gauze. Just fold it in several layers, cut out longer lines and sew them in some sort of laces and then sew it all together. Diana made a few of those for herself too.

There were different patients in their department. 'Thorax' in Latin means the part of a human body between the head and the abdomen. Most patients were with severe lung problems, the ones that could not be treated in Pulmonology anymore. There were patients with partial lung resection due to malignant growths detected at the late stages. She looked after those elderly men and took care of them always asking how they were and how they slept the previous night. All these men loved

Diana, some of them were saying that she would make a great doctor one day and that she had very gentle hands.

She loved her work and was asking nurses about different procedures that they did, always curious and keen to learn more. Some of the nurses were sceptic about Diana's necessity to study at all… "you know, your parents can get you anywhere you want, right?" But Diana was firm, and she knew her parents, they would never do anything like that, especially if it was about their own profession – surgery. If you wanted to become a doctor, you had no right to make mistakes. That was the attitude she knew from an early age. She was very serious about her job, even if it was mopping the floors and bringing bedpans to the patients after operations.

The same week that she started her new life in that hospital there arrived a young doctor for his residency training. He looked so hot in his scrubs. He was not tall, but he had very nice, tanned skin, big dark-brown eyes, and lips… the moment Diana saw him, she realized that she was not a little girl anymore… she wanted to kiss those lips, even if she had never done that before. So, whenever she saw him, she would turn all red and try to engage herself with something in the other part of the department.

She understood that it was her work, and there were rules, besides, everybody knew who her parents were. She knew how inappropriate it would be to do anything like that at work and just plunged into work with all her head.

In the mornings they would all gather at the head physician's office for their usual five-minute meetings, which never lasted five minutes, as they were discussing patients, and the aides were given their daily instructions too. Usually, it was about the number of operations on the floor and that they were to pick the patients from the operation unit to the ICU room. That meant that all her other daily routines must not interfere with that schedule.

The Intensive care unit was the place where people were mostly unconscious after their operations, and there were patients not only from the thoracal department – some were from urology and surgical departments. The nurses taught her how to change linen while the patient was in bed without disturbing him or her much, being also careful with all the tubes, sticking out of them. She was bringing water if patients asked her for it and if they were allowed to drink after the surgery, she was always checking that with the nurse on duty.

Once, some American doctors visited their city and brought a lot of medical stuff as part of their mission. There was glucose, disposable gowns for the operation units, I.V. sets, and some other bottles that nobody knew what they were. None of the staff knew English. Diana studied English at her school, and she really liked the language. So, she came up to the crowding doctors and nurses, who were standing in the corridor with some bottles in their hands and discussing something.

"What are you all doing here? What's there?"

"We were brought all this aid here to our hospital, but we don't understand what is what." Said the young doctor.

Diana blushed as usual when she interacted with him, then took a bottle and read.

"Sodium chloride – it's transparent, this is our normal saline solution, guys!" Diana smiled.

"You know English?" everybody wondered.

"A little." She smiled at them. Then she was given all the rest of the aid and was asked to sort everything out. Everybody recognized glucose though, it sounded the same in Russian. So, Diana was busy for a couple of days reading and sorting all the medications out. Then she noticed printed dates on the bottles with the abbreviated words before them "man." and "exp." She could not figure that out for a while as medical supplies in the Soviet Union were prepared in a different way, and usually, the dates were written in hand. And the bottles were different too. Soviet bottles were made of glass and the caps for them would be made of rubber, they would be covered with a piece of paper and 'sealed' with a rubber band. Not the firmest way to keep any solution of course, but they knew that everything was double-checked and handled with care. For example, glucose and saline solutions expired in thirty days, so, the label would contain the day of expiration only.

So, logically, Diana understood that man. stood for manufactured and exp. for expiration date. And then she realized that the expiration dates were longer on the foreign bottles. She came up with that to the head nurse. The American bottles were made of plastic and nurses were puzzled how to use them too. With time, everyone learnt how to work with them, and everything went in its usual way.

Once, one of the aides got ill and could not come to work, thus, there was nobody to stay for the night shift. Diana came up to the head nurse and asked if she could be the replacement. The nurse was one of the older staff, who also knew her parents. She knew that Diana was too young, and she did not want to get into trouble with her parents. But Diana persuaded the good woman, and she called her parents at the end of the workday and asked if she could stay in the hospital. Her mom did not want to show how worried she was and gave her consent without wishing 'good luck' as it was a sign of bad luck actually.

The night was calm. Most of the rest patients were already in the wards and were treated with regular infusions and injections. Nurses were changing bandages and looking after the healing process in general.

The main concern was the ICU patients, as they were recovering after operations. There were five beds in the intensive care ward and all of them were occupied. There were three men and two women. The women were just operated on in the evening and were still under anesthesia. One man was already conscious, but he had not gotten up yet after the operation. And the other two men were already in the full recovery process. One had an abdominal operation, and he was quite cheery, he chatted with Diana and praised her for her dexterity.

"You know, you are such a good girl. Keep going like that – study, achieve your goals, do not stop if you get into a wall just think about how to overcome it. Alright?" Mikhail would say.

"Ok, Mikhail. Thank you for your kind words. Do you need anything? I am finishing here for now, will go and wash the procedure room and the dressing ward as the nurses are done for today."

"No-no, Diana. I'm good. You are probably tired, you should have some rest too, you know." He said.

"I'm fine, young and strong! Don't worry about me. And I heard that you are going to be transferred tomorrow, isn't it great!" Diana smiled.

"Yeah, my children are also happy to hear that. They were worried about me, you know." He sighed.

"I can imagine. Though my parents are also doctors, they have their illnesses that they need to treat, and sometimes they get into hospitals as patients themselves. My brother and I had to do everything ourselves at home and then visit parents at the hospital when we were younger. Wasn't fun at all." Diana patted Mikhail's hand. "You should sleep now. Have some rest."

"Thank you, dear! Good night!"

During night shifts nurses and aides were divided into two groups: one group would work in the first part of the night and the other would change them after four–four-thirty in the morning. That was an unwritten rule that everybody followed. Diana was in the first group, so she cleaned everything after the busy day on their floor and around 2:30 went to the nurse's room to take a short nap. However, as it was her first working night, she was excited and overwhelmed with everything, so she could hardly tame her heart and make herself close her eyes.

Then another girl entered the room quietly. Diana was introduced to her before, but they never had a chance to talk. So, when Diana noticed that it was her, she opened her eyes and said "Hi."

"Oh, hi, I thought you were sleeping. You are that new girl, right? You look too young by the way. How old are you?"

"Ermm… sixteen. And you are Asem, right?"

"Yep. Why are you here? I heard your parents are doctors and half of the doctors here know them and you… Kinda awkward, don't you think?"

"Yeah… I know how it looks. But I really want to become a surgeon, and I asked my parents to let me work this summer."

"Ha-ha, I guess they have a plan."

"No-no, my brother used to work in one of these hospitals too, and now he is at the medical university."

"Oh, you are considering it seriously then. I'm here just temporarily. I'm a student at a pedagogical university. Going to be a teacher in the future." Asem said nonchalantly.

"Oh, I see. How long have you been working here?"

"Every summer and I take night shifts now and then. Convenient, you know. And the pay is good. I'll graduate in a year, fingers crossed."

"Oh, this is my first job ever. I've never earned any money before," Diana said with a smile.

"Are you planning to sleep tonight?" Asem interrupted.

"Well, I'm too excited, not sleepy at all."

"Ok, then. Let's get out of here. Nurses will come here too; they will have more room on the sofa then."

And they went out to the staircase and chatted until dawn sitting on a windowsill.

Asem told her a story about her friend who was kidnapped the previous summer. And by kidnapping, she meant that it was some guy, who liked that girl and decided that she would be his wife. And instead of wooing her properly and going out like a normal person would do, he decided to do it in an ancient way – kidnap the bride. Diana could not believe her ears. XX century out there and some people were still doing some crazy stuff from the times of yore…

"This is ridiculous and outrageous! What did her parents do? Where is she now?"

"Oh, don't worry! Your friend here arranged a whole rescue operation. We chased the guy on a motorbike of my friend!"

"Wow! And?"

"The guy lived in some village and the girl was from town. So, we realized that he would take the road that we had expected him to take, so we got there faster. We were speeding and were actually stopped by the road militia, but we started explaining to them and ask them to help us stop that crime. Because it was a crime against a human! Oh, man! I can't believe that I was so daring to talk like that to those militia guys. At first, they refused, as they knew that some people were still following such dumb traditions, but I was very persuasive!" Asem beamed as she said that.

Diana was looking at her with admiration:

"Wow! You are awesome! And? What did the militia do?"

"Oh, they stopped the car, as if for speeding or something, and while they were checking their documents, we dashed to the car, opened the back door, and took my friend out! Can you imagine, they put a pillowcase on her head! Unbelievable!"

"Oh, my!"

"Good thing was that our motorbike had a sidecar body, so we put my friend there, covered her, and just drove away into the sunset!"

"Cool!"

"So, the girl studies at the university alright. And her destiny could be completely different, you know... She would have probably had babies by now and would be cleaning and washing the dishes all day long in her in-laws' house."

Diana was speechless. She never heard stories like that and that was happening in her own hometown. Crazy!

"Hey, the day is breaking already, we should really get some sleep. You are staying for the day shift too, right? That's a 32 hour-working day. You should rest. So, let's go. We still have a couple of hours."

And they went to the nurses' room and lay on the sofa. One of the nurses was up already and left the room.

In an hour she woke up as if she was startled by something. She could not understand what it was, but it was not a good thing. All the nurses were gone from that room and Asem was gone too. Diana came out to the corridor and looked. There were people in the ICU. She ran up there thinking that probably one of the female patients had some complications after the surgery. But when she entered the ward, Mikhail's bed was empty, and she heard the cargo lift moving down.

"What's going on? Where is Mikhail? He was fine, right? He is transferred already?"

"Diana..." Asem said quietly.

"What? What happened here?"

"Listen, this happens sometimes. He had some serious complications after the surgery."

"But his surgery was like three days ago. He was fine!"

"Yeah, this happens." Asem was holding her hand and trying to calm Diana down with her firmness.

"But how? His children are going to come today!" Diana sobbed.

"He had a malignant tumor, and the operation was aimed at cutting it out, but he had metastatic lesions in different organs... I just read it in his records."

"But he was so cheerful yesterday. I talked to him, we laughed!"

"Yeah, consider it as agony, dear. You need to calm down. Go wash your face with cold water. You must not show this to other patients. This is oncology. All the patients here are anxious and if you come up to them with tears in your eyes, they would take it to their heart. Now, go."

Diana left the room. Other patients were not aware of what was happening there. Still asleep or unconscious.

That was the first time when the person she knew died, though she did not see his body. She wanted to cry, and tears were welling up in her eyes during the day, but she was holding up well.

There was another man in the ICU, who was also to be transferred to a ward for recovery that day. His name was Oleg. He was tall and seemed to be doing well. He was getting up already and his daughter visited him, and he went for a little walk in the yard in front of the hospital with her.

It was four in the afternoon. All the patients had their lunch and were napping in the afternoon. Diana was preparing a usual snack and a drink for the patients. She felt the exhaustion now and regretted not sleeping more the previous night. She was anticipating the end of the workday, which was in less than an hour for her. But usually, she would stay longer to talk to the other shift and give them details about different patients.

As she was making another round to pick up the cups and plates from the patients, she entered the ICU and felt that something was wrong. Oleg was lying straight on his back, and he was so still and yellow. That could not be right. Diana came up to him trying to shake his shoulder, but he did not respond. She checked his pulse on the neck – nothing.

"No! Not another one!" Diana thought and ran out to call a doctor or a nurse.

She knew that she was not supposed to panic, and she tried to be as calm as possible and tell everything to the doctors in the on-call room. They all went to the ICU and the doctors pronounced him dead.

And again! Diana could not understand and would not want to believe that a person could walk and be cheerful and then just die. There were other nurses in the room now and Diana tried to act professionally. She asked what she was to do and then followed all the instructions she was given without a sob.

She could not talk when she came home. Her mother told her to take a nap before dinner as she was working so long. But Diana was so frustrated and empty, that she could not even cry or sleep. She just lay in bed and looked into the ceiling. Now she understood her father, who used to work there, and he was probably losing his patients like that sometimes, probably walking through every step he did during the operation and then afterwards, trying to find the flaw. But sometimes, whatever you do, if it is this man's destiny and his time is up, no doctor will be able to save his life.

With these thoughts, Diana lapsed into a dreamless sleep.

After that Diana was taking a few night shifts and a 24-hour shift for some weekends now and then. She was still enjoying her work and valuing life even more.

Sometimes she was taken aback by the men who had just had their right lung removed, for example, as she would catch them smoking in the men's toilet.

"Oh, uncle Alexey, why are you doing this? You have just one lung left; don't you want to keep it healthy?"

"Diana, dear! I love it when you call me uncle!"

"Don't change the subject, please!"

"Oh, come on. We live just once and I was smoking all my life, and I know that I will never quit, so…"

She was angry with such an attitude.

"But doctors were fighting for your life here and they were taking care of you… and you… you just bring all their efforts to naught!"

"Alright, alright. Here, I put it down. And I am leaving… See?"

"Thank you!"

During the three months that she worked there, she saw so many people with the worst consequences from smoking that it made her hate smoking even more, as she never liked the smell of it anyway.

One morning Diana came to work, and she saw some agitation in the department. Turned out there was an urgent operation at night and the man just woke up. He was loud, and by the sound, she could understand that he was aggressive too!

By mutual decision, he was transferred to a separate ward 4 at the end of the corridor. All the necessary equipment was brought there from the ICU by the aides and the room was set.

When the man was transferred, Diana saw that he was not that old and that surprised her because the average age of the patients in that department was around fifty. That guy was in his thirties. Later Diana peeped into his hospital chart and found out that he was thirty-three. For some reason, nurses were giving her a lot of errands that did not include ward 4. She was perplexed and wanted to ask someone about it. And the man was always loud and aggressive, even after he was off the strong painkillers or maybe because of that...

She heard nurses whisper things about him, and she realized that some of them might be true. As she saw him in the corridor, his upper body that was visible to everybody in the corridor was all covered in tattoos. And as it was 1992, those were some specific tattoos, not the ones that you can make at a salon today.

The one that she saw on his shoulder was "I'll never forget my mom". A very clear message from a place of exile. Diana was shocked again... he was comparatively young and judging by the number of such tattoos, he was in jail not once.

Anyway, one day she was the only one left in the department, who could wash the floors and everything in his room. Before going there, the on-call doctor and a nurse gave her very clear instructions:

"Do not come up too close to him. Put on several masks, he has an active form of Tuberculosis, your parents are gonna kill us if they find out that we sent you to him!"

"My lips are sealed! Don't worry! I'll do everything quickly and leave."

"Also, try not to talk to him and do not listen to him much, he swears a lot. And you, poor thing, are too young even to hear such things."

"Oh, come on, I'm alright, as if I don't know swear words!" Diana flaunted.

"Ok, just be careful. He's aggressive."

So, Diana prepared the dusters, the disinfection solution, the bucket, and her mop, put on three masks on her face, which looked weird, she realized that, but who would want to deal with the active TB form?

As she entered the room, she smelt some unbearable stench. The man opened his eyes, squinted, and stared at her for a while.

"I haven't seen you before. Are you new?"

Diana ignored him and just wiped the surfaces.

"Are you deaf, you little bitch?"

Diana blushed as she was never sworn at by an adult. It felt wrong and weird.

"Oh, look, she is hiding like behind two-three masks? Are you afraid of me? Huh? What did they say to you? That I'm some narc from the prison?"

Diana was wiping the windowsill trying to stay calm.

"If I was in prison, it doesn't mean that I am worthless!" he started yelling. "I worked as a welder and that's why my lungs are rotting now… I'm spitting out my lungs, did you know that? You, pussy! I know that I'm gonna fucking die soon, as it ain't no good if you are spitting your lungs out, right, you bitch?"

Diana was shocked and her ears were ringing, but she continued cleaning without showing her reaction.

Then the patient pulled down the blanket and started opening his bandages trying to show her the cuts after the operation.

"This ain't look good, right?"

Diana glanced at it and was aghast. His bandages seemed fresh, but the inside of it was all greenish, as the cut was obviously leaking. She ran out of the ward to call the nurse and heard him yelling:

"You, fucking wuss!"

As they returned, he already opened all his bandages and was breathing heavily, muttering some curses to no one in particular.

Diana looked at him and she pitied the man. She was not scared; it was his defensive reaction. He was obviously scared… He was still young and wanted to live more.

Later, when she was back to school, she met Asem in the street, and she told her that Anatoly died in September after another operation.

Those three months that she worked, she really loved the job, the people, the patients, and the incredible efforts that doctors made in order to save anyone's life. And she made a decision for herself.

It was almost the end of August when she said to her parents during the dinner:

"I decided what surgeon I want to be."

"Mhm?" Her dad looked at her chewing the meat.

"I want to be like you, dad, an oncological surgeon. That's where you really matter! You can really save someone's life there!"

Her dad stopped chewing. He slowly swallowed the meat and then said:

"Are you aware that people also die on the operation table, and what's worse, after a successful operation too."

"I know... I saw that. And it's sad. But I really want to do something meaningful in my life."

"But... but we thought that this job in oncology will scare you away from the medicine." Her mom said quietly.

"Nope. If I were scared, I would have run away from there in June, but I'm still there."

"What about your allergies? They keep coming up and we never know what you will react to next?"

"I know, but what else can I do? I grew up listening to your stories about patients, about you saving someone's life and it was always so inspiring..."

"Darling, we know... but don't rush with your decisions, ok? You still have time, maybe you will change your mind?"

"But I don't want to change my mind!" Diana raised her voice.

The next day, she went to work as usual. Greeted everyone from the night shift, asked the news about the patients as usual. Exchanged a few jokes with Sulen, the handsome doctor, laughed and felt comfortable about it.

She usually had lunch with the hospital matron – a tiny woman in her fifties. Her name was Nina, and she was very active and curious. Diana talked to her sometimes when they were alone. So that day, she decided to share her parents' point of view. Besides, Nina knew her father very well.

"Oh, I understand them. No parent would want such a darned job like that for their child!" she said casually.

"What? Why? This is the noblest job ever! They save people's lives!"

"And?"

"What and? You don't understand!"

"Darling, I worked here all my life… I saw death hundreds of times, though I am not even a real nurse. Do you think I wanted to be here?"

"Why? What did you want to be then?"

"Seriously, you don't think that I dreamed to become a hospital matron as a child. I wanted to be a ballerina!"

"What? Wow! What happened then?" Diana looked at her concerned.

"Well, my mother was telling me that I was the most talented ballet dancer ever and that I would be prima in Bolshoi theatre one day. And that I should go to Moscow and enter the ballet dance school there after the ordinary school here. I was an A student, and everyone was admiring me!" a glimpse of dreaminess appeared in the usually dull eyes of the woman.

"What happened then?" Diana was trying to explain to herself what could have happened if the dancer of a great promise ended up in a hospital in a small town.

"Well, I went to Moscow alright, and I went to the auditions. I prepared several dances too. I wasn't worried about academic exams – Russian and Literature were my favourites. I passed those alright. But the admissions committee did not like my dance. They said that my movements were angular or something and that I did not listen to the music… and something else, I don't remember."

"And?" Diana was looking at her inquiringly.

"And… they told me to come the next year and try again, because, as they said I was conveniently tiny." She chuckled.

"And? What happened when you tried again?"

"I came home, and I had nothing to do. My mother was disappointed in me, as I have never failed before. She said that I should look for a job that would feed me until I go and try again."

"And?"

"Almost thirty-five years passed since then… I could never make myself go there and try again. I was afraid of that humiliation that I had to experience. And my mother did not make it easier. If before she was only praising me for my excellent skills in anything I did, now she was only pointing at my drawbacks: I was too skinny, I was too bony that no man would ever look at me... and she was right. I am fifty-three now and I was never married, darling."

Diana was in a state of complete prostration.

"Why didn't you go? Why didn't you prove your mother wrong?" she was steaming.

"I just couldn't, you know... "

"But what about other colleges or universities? If you were an excellent student, you could go anywhere, right?"

"Right... I was scared of failure. But you... You should look at all the opportunities your life will suggest to you! Promise me that you will never stop, even if medicine will not be your future."

"But I want to be a doctor!"

"Then go and work in a clinic, but not here. There is death here in every corner..."

"I know, I am ready for that."

"No, it's just your bravado, kid." She sighed. "Look, you learn languages, you are an excellent student too. As you said, you can choose any university. Don't limit yourself. You never know what life is keeping for you. Ok?"

For the rest few days of her work at the hospital, Diana kept looking at Nina and felt the bitterness of the unrealized life of that tiny woman. She remembered that conversation for the rest of her life.

One year passed and after a million and one discussions with her parents she easily entered another university and chose another profession. So, in the family of doctors there appeared a teacher of English... for a change.

A Train Story

August 1994

It was four in the morning in August. Chilly northern air was stirring the travelers' hair giving them the last goodbye kiss before they set off to the south, where summer was still in full reign. The dark sky forbode coming later in the day rain, which made some leaving people a little bit relieved. They knew exactly that in some thirty hours they would be wearing shorts and t-shirts again instead of warm fleece jackets and jumpers, thus prolonging their own summer. You know, every northerner's dream.

The train arrived at Platform 2. Nobody was happy about it, as they had to cross the railway through the bridge, which was too much of a trouble, so most people were just walking and dragging their luggage over the rails of the first platform. The guard was not even whistling at people for that. After all, it was 4 am and there were only two trains coming to town that night.

Diana was travelling alone for the first time and her dad was genuinely worried about that. He kept giving her instructions on what to do and what not to do on the train and how not to forget her stuff when getting off the train in Almaty. Diana was a bit sleepy, but at the same time so overly excited that she simply could not hear what her father was saying. She was anticipating all sorts of adventures that might happen to her when she arrived in the big city. She might go out somewhere, maybe with her cousins and meet some new people and maybe finally meet a young man, who would become her future husband... yeah, just like that.

In the meantime, the train arrived on time, and everybody started making their way to their carriages.

"Carriage 15, compartment IV, seat 15, that's a lower bank, ok?" her dad was carrying her bag quickly walking along the moving train. "It should stop somewhere near the bridge, so go there and look for the number plate in the window."

"Ok, dad, don't you worry." She said absent-mindedly.

She was seventeen and she just finished her first year at the university with straight A's, and this trip was some sort of a reward for her efforts. She was also worried about what to do on the train, as she remembered their family trips and they were always fun because her older brother was with her. He would make up some games and they would play them all twenty-eight hours of their journey, with a little break for sleep. She hated sleeping in trains. But the games were really fun. They would count electric poles on each side of the road, so you needed to pick a side first and then just stand at the window and count out loud. I guess their parents loved that game! Imagine two over-pumped with energy kids simply standing and counting poles... Sometimes it could be trees if they were passing the steppe area. Not many of those there, you know. Counting sheep and cows was another game. Or looking at the clouds and figuring out what they looked like! And Diana's imagination was great! She would see a polar bear, or a camel, or a turtle, or that Olympic bear from Moscow 1980!

Now she felt all grown-up and she was going to Almaty all by herself. No games... just new adventures and new life!

As you understand, there were no mobile phones yet, so you can feel the worry of her father. As soon as the train stopped and the door of the carriage was opened, he came up to the carriage conductor and asked to look after his daughter, showed him the ticket and they shook hands.

Diana was not paying attention to details, her mind was already far away, indulging in adventures.

The compartment was almost full, her bunk was supposed to be below and empty, but to her father's and her own surprise, it was occupied by someone, who was deeply sleeping and snoring loudly. She put her bag under the table and came out to say goodbye to dad. He was still grumpy about her seat, and Diana said that it was fine and that she could climb up and sleep on the second shelf. That calmed her dad down a little. It was time for departure, so she pecked her dad on his cheek and hugged him.

* * *

It was pitch dark and stuffy in the compartment. And the sonorous snore of her bunk intruder was filling the night air so much that it was even difficult to hear her own thoughts. Diana could switch on the lights to see if the bed was made, but she thought better of it and decided not to wake the neighbours up. Despite the fact that she was pretty tired already, she decided to get out of that stuffiness and deafening snore into the corridor.

As it was summer, the windows in the train were not sealed, so you could open them and breathe the fresh air in. And that was what she did. The cool wind was blowing straight into her head, making her long hair messy. She was just looking into the dark sky, trying to count stars and dream…

The sun in the steppe rises early. One can see the solar fireball above the horizon around five – five-thirty in the morning. The haze around it looks mystic and reminds you of the scenes from a desert in Africa on National Geographic.

The picture was majestic, and Diana's eyes swelled up with tears… or, maybe it was just wind that dried her eyes a little. She could hear birds chirping and playfully trying to chase the train. The world was waking up and she was relishing the beauty of it catching those first rays on her face.

Around seven in the morning a young man came out of compartment IV and headed for the toilet. He had a towel on his shoulder and a toothbrush with a tube of toothpaste in his hand. She did not pay much attention to him as the morning was bright already and the sun was spreading its rays all over the steppe, making the yellowish grass in the fields look not so pathetic.

The carriage conductor boiled the tea at the entrance of the carriage, and the early-bird people were getting ready for breakfast. The young man returned and smiled at her as he passed by to his compartment. She decided to look inside too, after all her stuff was inside and she did not even see her bunk. To the man's surprise, she followed him in. She smiled and said:

"Hello, I'm actually your neighbour. Just don't like to sleep in trains."

"Hello to you!" he laughed. "That explains it."

"Pardon?"

"Well, I woke up and saw the bags. I know that this elderly man put his bags under his bunk, and our bags are under my sister's seat… so I was wondering who could be our mysterious fourth companion."

"I'm not mysterious at all. Just did not want to wake any of you up in the middle of the night." Diana laughed. "Besides, my bunk is this, not the upper one…" she continued lowering her voice.

"Oh, gee… That man took your place, how disgraceful of him!" The man laughed back in a low voice. "Anyway, as soon as they wake up, let's have breakfast. You eat in trains, right?"

Diana laughed again "Oh yeah. I eat."

'Mm, two minutes talking, and he made me laugh twice already… interesting…' she thought to herself. 'Maybe my adventures will start earlier after all?'

Interestingly enough, she did not feel shy at all, she felt so natural with him, and it felt good.

She went to the toilet too, brushed her teeth, and combed her disarrayed hair. She had some food in the bag: sandwiches and fried chicken. As soon as all the people in the carriage woke up, they started preparing for breakfast, some were getting off at the next station, so they were carrying their bags closer to the door. There was that general clamour and the rhythmical chugging of the train that created that peculiar atmosphere, making Diana feel like she was in some sort of a dream with the train rocking her gently.

At breakfast, all the four people in compartment IV introduced themselves to each other. The young man's name was Bulat, his sister was Ulzhan, and the elderly man was Rakhim aga. He was apologizing for taking Diana's bunk, but she was ok with that, as she respected old people and would never allow a person in such a respectful age to climb on the upper bunk.

All of them put all the food they had on the table and shared it with each other. They talked and laughed. Rakhim aga was telling some jokes about his elderly wife, but they could feel how much he loved her, and it was so sweet. He was visiting his children in Petropavlovsk and was going back to Karaganda to his wife.

"Please eat all these baursaks[1], kids, otherwise my wife will be grumbling that I did not eat anything again." He said.

"But you really didn't eat much, aga!" Bulat exclaimed. "Let me bring you some tea."

"Oh, thank you, dear. I love tea. By the way, kiddo, I guess you are younger than your sister, right?"

"Yeah, how do you know?" Bulat stopped at the door. They were both in their twenties, but you could not be sure who was older between the two of them.

"Well, your sister's name is Ulzhan, means 'son's soul', did you know that?" He looked at the girl.

She nodded, chewing baursak with a boiled egg.

"So, Kazakhs gave girls such names as Ulzhan, Ulbala, Ulbolsyn, Ulmeken[2] hoping to have a son someday. It's a superstition of course, but somehow it works. See?" He smiled and winked at Bulat.

"That's interesting, aga!" Diana smiled.

"Good that you learned something new today!" the old man smiled again.

---

[1] Baursaks - Kazakh national dish, fried pieces of dough
[2] Ulbala, Ulbolsyn, Ulmeken – direct translation of the names - baby boy, let it be a boy and is it a boy.

One hour later, in Karaganda, Rakhim aga got off the train, but he gave his sumptuous blessings to all the young people of his compartment before he left.

* * *

The more to the south the train moved, the warmer it was getting in the train and outside. Diana did not like to sit in the stuffy compartment, so she came out to the corridor again, looking at the dull scenery. This time Bulat came out too and stood next to her. It was awkward to stand there in silence, so Diana tried to furtively peek at him and see if she actually liked him. The response in her guts was positive and she smiled.

"What? Do I have food on my face?" Bulat asked smiling. "By the way, that old man was so much fun, he reminded me of our grandfather."

"Yeah, same here and no, there is no food on your face. I just thought that it was awkward to stand like that in silence."

"Hmm... yeah. So, let's talk. There is nothing else to do here."

"Let's!" Diana willingly agreed.

"How old are you?"

"17. You?"

"24."

'Oh, old...' Diana thought with regret.

"What are you doing? Studying anywhere?"

"Yeah, pedagogical university. Going to be an English teacher. What about you?"

"Ooh, nice. I graduated from Polytechnical institute last year, served almost two years in the army too."

"Wow, interesting. Did you like it in the army?"

"Not really, why are you asking?"

"Well, as a child I wanted to be a boy and go to the army when I grow up."

"My turn to say 'Wow'..." he smiled.

"And why didn't you like it? Doesn't it help you develop strong character?"

"Oh, you like a strong character. Well, one drunk officer was jokingly playing with his gun and accidentally shot me. I was just doing my duties and he got me. Definitely did not enjoy that part."

"Really? That's horrible! Where did he wound you?"

"Ok, I can show." And he lifted his pants and showed the calf on his right leg. Part of the muscle was missing as if someone snatched a piece of it out.

"Oh my God, does it still hurt?" she asked with compassion.

"Ah, no… It's alright now." He smiled again looking into her eyes with interest.

"You know, I wanted to become a surgeon, but my parents were against that idea."

"Why? Surgeons are cool!"

"I know, both my parents are surgeons, and my brother studies at the medical institute too, but they do not want me to be like them… so, I had to choose something different." She sighed.

"You seem not to like your specialty. But you are still young, you can do what you want in your life."

"Thanks for that, but I do like the idea of teaching. So, I guess, everything is for the better."

And they talked like that for hours. They had tea around seven in the evening and went out of the compartment to continue talking. Ulzhan smiled at her brother when they were leaving the compartment again.

The train was squeaking and rattling as if trying to interrupt those two telling its own story of its endless trips all around the country. It was not a surprise for the train to see two young people bonding so much and so closely, as there were thousands of similar stories that it could tell them.

Time stopped for them, they were discussing books, films, professions, the president, and the future of their young country and how much hopes they had about it. Diana felt so free and natural with him, she started having another feeling about him. Her inner judge was opening her eye, whispering:

"Are you out of your mind? He's like a hundred years older than you… and where is he going? Maybe he is going to his fiancée and just not telling you about her. Men are mean!"

"Shut up! He's just seven years older than me and he is awesome!" she was reasoning with herself while listening to another story that Bulat was telling her so passionately. "Just look at him, he is a good man!"

Around one o'clock after midnight Ulzhan looked out of the compartment:

"You two are still talking? Hehe, didn't know that you can talk so much, Bulat." She looked at her brother and smiled. "Anyway, I want to sleep. We arrive at 7:38 am, so… Night-night."

"Good night, Ulzhan. Sorry, Bulat, I can talk like that for ages, you know. But you need to sleep, you go." Diana smiled back at them both.

"No, I want to stay awhile. Night, sis." He said and looked at Diana. "So, what were we talking about?"

"Oh, so many things…" she said.

They looked around the carriage, the lights were deemed already, people were sleeping, and they did not even notice that.

"Wow, it's really late and it seemed like an hour."

"Yeah, tell me about it." She smiled and looked into the darkness outside. In fact, she was piercing into Bulat's reflection in the window. He was tall and handsome, well-built, and he had smooth olive skin. His hair was dark and short, and his eyes were deep brown, just like hers. She noticed that when they started talking in the morning when he was a stranger to her, but by the night he became someone, with whom she would like to spend more time together.

She felt that he was close to her, their thighs were touching and rubbing against each other with the rhythm of the train. And though it was the second night in a row when she did not sleep, she was more than alert. She had that insomnia since her high school years and was used to it. She could sit all night looking into the dark sky, dreaming about the future, or writing some verses in English, which she could not read to anyone in her environment.

The train chugged and chew-chewed and she was swaying in that rhythm feeling so content and excited because it was one of her dreams to talk all day and night with someone, who would understand her completely. And here he was. Right next to her.

Their hands touched each other accidentally as the train made a marcato in its dull flow of the melody. Diana felt as if she was electrocuted and that made her hold her breath for a second. She closed her eyes and exhaled… and then she felt his hand touching her hair. She turned her head to him trying to breathe evenly. He looked at her neck and then into her eyes. Gently he moved closer and kissed her lightly into her neck. Another shockwave ran through her body.

"Oh my, what's going on?" was her last thought.

"I wanted to do this for a while now…" he said quietly. His face was buried into her hair; she felt his hot breath on her neck suspecting that she was losing her senses. His hand reached her hand and another wave of electrocution…

Her eyes were half-closed, and she was hardly breathing now, her heart was pounding so loudly, and it seemed that something inside her chest was about to burst into millions of pieces of light and spread around the carriage, then the train and the steppe and then reach the endless sky…

"Wha…" she wanted to ask him what he wanted to do when he started kissing her innocent lips.

That light inside her was spilling all over her body, filling in every inch of it, making her warm and trembling.

He looked at her surprised and delighted.

"Have you ever kissed a man?" he whispered.

"No…" she whispered back.

"Oh, you are amazing." He devoured her with his eyes in that deemed light. "Let's go to the covered platform, there is more air there."

"Let's…"

And she followed him, holding his hand, feeling silly and happy. They just clicked. And all she needed to do was just get on that train. Who could know?

They kissed and talked until the first passengers, those early-birds, started waking up and getting ready for their final station. They decided not to shock the public and retreat to the compartment, where Ulzhan was already waking up too.

"You two were up all night? Why can't you just sleep like normal people?" she was a bit grumpy in the morning.

"Don't pay attention to my old grumpy sister, she likes to sleep… a lot." And he winked at Diana.

She smiled and realized how swollen her lips were from all the kissing. But it was still dark and Ulzhan could not see that, however, she felt that something was definitely different between these two sleepless in the train.

"Ok, let's have some tea before we arrive." She mumbled sleepily.

They were to gather and submit the sheets and pillowcases that conductors provided the passengers with and gather their own stuff before they left the train. Diana drank some water; she was too excited to eat after such a night.

Bulat was looking at her now and then, smiling and trying to make it unnoticeable to his sister. Diana and Ulzhan were chatting about different things before they arrived at Almaty station. And Bulat and Diana never thought how they were going to communicate when they leave the train.

The moment the train stopped, he was struck by that thought and looked for a piece of paper and a pen or a pencil to write his phone number down. Diana was turning around to have another look at the man of her dreams when he slipped that piece of paper into her hand. Her hands were full. She had so many bags with presents for her relatives in town, whom she was visiting. And there was another bag with her clothes, so she grasped the paper and smiled thankfully at Bulat, as she was too shy to ask for his number. The mess and the crowd at the exit of the carriage, all those people with luggage, everything was so hectic. She thought of giving one of her aunt's phone numbers to him, but she did not remember them by heart, she had to take out her notebook to get it, but the crowd was already carrying her out of the train and away from it, and away from her Bulat.

That same crowd brought her to the bus stop, and they all got on a bus that was going to her aunts' place. She tried to look for Bulat or Ulzhan in that crowd and realized that they were taking another bus to another part of the big city. She wanted to wave at him, but her hands were still occupied; her heart was warm as she knew that she had his phone number now. She checked her right hand, which was almost purple because of the weight of the bags, there was nothing... Then she looked at her left hand and... the piece of paper with the number was GONE... she probably lost it when she was getting on the bus, or maybe somewhere on the way... Did it really matter? She lost the only thread that could connect them. The lump in her throat was treacherously stifling her, making her sob. Her eyes were filled with bitter tears, and she did not know what to do.

"He doesn't even know that I lost it... and he will be waiting for my call..." she thought swallowing her tears and sniffing with her runny nose.

"Are you alright, dear?" asked a woman, who was sitting next to her. Diana was standing with her bags in her hands, balancing without holding any rails and crying in that stuffed bus.

"No, I am not..." and sobbed again.

"Do you want to sit down?" the kind woman inquired.

"No, I'm ok. Thank you."

When she got home to her grandmother's, one of her aunts saw her red eyes and asked if everything was alright on the way there. Diana told her the whole story and cried again. Her aunt was at a loss, trying to comfort her, suggesting looking for him somehow.

"But I don't even know his last name..."

"Oh, that's complicated then..." her aunt sighed.

"Yeah... I'll be fine." Diana sobbed, inhaled, and slowly exhaled. She said that more to herself than to the aunt.

* * *

Many years passed since that journey. Diana grew into a beautiful woman. After her first university, she went to Almaty to get her master's degree in business administration. She married then a guy from her course and they had three wonderful kids together. They divorced after a while and the children were living with her. She worked in an oil company and then as a teacher of English at a university in Almaty, and her children were visiting their father in Astana every school break. Sometimes she went to Astana with them and visited her uncle there.

One day, on the way back she passed the registration and passport control and went on board the plane. She asked the lady to give her a seat at the window, as the flight was not long. Usually, she would sit and watch a film or read a book if there were no screens on the plane. This time she was going to read a detective story. Passengers were filling up the salon, placing their bags above seats and fastening belts as soon as they settled down. Someone approached her row asking if that was row fifteen, she nodded without looking up and continued reading.

When the aircraft was gaining speed on the runway, Diana closed her eyes and started whispering a prayer as she usually did. Her hands were on the handles, and then she felt someone's hand on hers; she automatically jerked it away saying "sorry".

The man next to her was staring at her with all his eyes not believing himself. She noticed the look and felt uncomfortable.

"I'm sorry, you know, I don't feel comfortable when the plane rises in the air."

"Nobody likes that, you bet."

She turned her head to look at the man.

"It's you... It's actually you..." his voice cracked in disbelief.

"B-bulat? Oh my..." Tears filled her eyes just like the last time when she saw him... thirty years ago.

"Why didn't you call me? I was waiting for your call all the time we were in Almaty. My sister thought I have lost my mind. She said that I would forget you very soon... But I never did."

"You won't believe it, but I lost that piece of paper somewhere at the train station when the crowd was carrying me away from you. I realized that only on the bus and I saw you and Ulzhan at the bus stop, waiting for another bus going in some other direction. I cried and did not know what to do, where to look for you. We talked so much, but we never mentioned where we were going to stay in Almaty. Neither you, nor me."

"Yeah, I realized how dumb I was then, that I let you go without taking your number..."

"But here we are now..."

"Yeah, here we are…"

"How have you been? Are you married? Children? Work? Where do you live?" she was that seventeen-year-old girl again. "Sorry, too many questions… still can't believe it… It's you!!!"

"At first it was tough, I kept thinking about you. I started learning English because of you, you know…"

"Oh, that's sweet."

"Then I had to pull myself together. I met a girl, we got married, we did not have children for a long time and then we decided to adopt."

"Oh, how noble of you. Go on."

"We took a boy from the village, you know, he is actually my relative. His parents died and he was living with his old grandparents. So, we took him and raised him, he is a student now. I'm proud of him. My wife and I decided to divorce after fifteen years of marriage. This happens, you know."

"I know…" she said with some sort of relief.

"You know?"

"Yeah. Go on…"

"I'm a civil engineer, worked in Astana for a long time, and after divorce, I moved to Almaty. What about you?"

"Wow, I can't believe it… You're in Almaty. I live in Almaty too now. And of course, you have a girlfriend or someone?"

"Not really… Women get suspicious when they meet a single man in his fifties."

"Do they?"

"Oh yeah… So, back to you, madame, did you end up becoming a teacher? Or a surgeon after all?"

"Oh no… Life is a funny thing. I am a translator now and a writer…" she paused. "How foolish we were not even asking our last names!"

"Yeah, and home phones of our parents at least, or something. It's so much easier today… By the way, can I have your phone now? All phone numbers that you have, please… I don't say that usually to anyone, but you were the best and miraculous thing that ever happened to me!"

"Really?"

"I'm so happy that I bought this ticket, you can't imagine how difficult it is to look for Diana without any other characteristics in our country, where Diana is a very popular name, you know…"

"I know… I know…" she took his hand into hers and that same wave ran through her once again, as if those long thirty years never existed. "I am divorced and have three children, by the way. Will that scare you away from me?"

"Nothing will scare me away from you now…" he smiled gently kissing her hand.

"But we are not those young and careless kids anymore…"

"I know… for me you will always be that girl from the train. Oh, Ulzhan would be crazy to hear about that!"

"Oh, my…" she smiled. "Ulzhan, your sis, right… Would you like to have some tea in town after we land?"

"Can't wait…"

They took one taxi and he called her on her phone so that she would save his number too. They were both so exhilarated with that encounter, still not believing, holding hands, and looking into each other's eyes, that the taxi driver thought that they were newlyweds.

They giggled, just like thirty years ago they were laughing at each other's jokes and stories, talking about the future and their dreams all day and night long, and they did not want to lose each other ever again.

A Vision

It was the 27th of April on the calendar. Diana got up at 6 am as usual to get her children ready for school. When she entered the kitchen, she looked at the clock and then at the calendar as-a-matter-of-factly, frowned a little saying to herself: "Oh, it's 27th already, Thursday… well, time flies! Soon it's your daughter's birthday, you need to get her a present… Let me think, what would she accept with joy? Of course, she wants to have an iPad and it's not a secret at all. Ok, I'll think about it later, as Scarlett O'Hara would say… well, 27th – a good date, a good day… to die… what? What's that about? How did this phrase appear in my head at all? But I definitely heard it somewhere… this expression… Probably, some action movie. I don't know. Oh, it doesn't matter. Think of the breakfast. What would you do to feed your little sharks? Ok then, omelet – delicious and healthy".

With the usual moves she hit one egg at the edge of the bowl, pouring the essence into it, then the second one, poured some milk, churned it with the whisk, and put some salt, while the pan was already getting hot on the stove. She poured sunflower oil into it, still stirring the mix in the bowl, and when she saw that oil drops started chasing each other on the black surface of the pan, she poured the omelet mix into it and made the heat less on her electric ceramic stove.

"Ok, now the main part – wake up girls… How I don't like to do it… they are so sweet when they sleep. I would have watched them for ages. But… got to go… gotta go gotta go!!!"

On entering the girls' room, she looked at it over critically. Scattered clothes on one side of the room and accurately piled clothes on the other. "How come they are so different? All righty, I'm turning on the lights" she sighed smiling at her thoughts.

"Girls, get up! Come on, wake up… It's morning, the sun is high, the grass is green, birds are singing. I am opening your duvets, and yes, I know how cozy and warm it is snuggling under them. But it's totally your own fault if you didn't have enough sleep, as you were whispering till it was reeeaally late. That's it! Get up! Hop-hop! Go! Go! Go! Come on girls, show me how you can dress very quickly." the mommy was making so much noise that girls had to get up eventually.

Ailene sat in her bed, screwing up her eyes looking at their agile mom:

"Come on, say that if we are not dressed in five minutes, then you won't comb our hair and make braids…"

"That's right!" said Diana.

"Ma, we are not kids anymore. We can do it ourselves… Even Jane. And why do you always wake us up so early? I can go like this, without any stupid plaits." the last words she said more to herself, as she knew that her mom was losing temper when she saw them uncombed or with loose hair.

"Ok, honey, stop grumbling. You got up, that's great! Go and wash your face now! And what about you? Why are you still in bed? What are you waiting for? Come on, Jane, pumpkin, get up." she said that patting the back of her second daughter and kissing her on her sleepy brown-greenish eyes, who was still slugging in the bed, trying to wake up. "Come on, ladies, you know that there may be traffic jams on the roads, and your school is not that close. Put on clothes and march to the kitchen. Your bus is arriving in thirty minutes."

"Why don't you take us to school yourself?" asked Jane whining as usual in the mornings.

"You know, honey, I need to take your little brother to the nursery, and it is in the opposite direction from your school. I just can't do that, I am sorry, sweetie. And I have so many things to do in the city. I need to get to several places before you come home. And, besides, this house needs to be cleaned too, and you eat every day… So, I am cooking too. What do you say to that?"

Jane bit her lip; she was about to burst out crying. Diana hated such moments. But Jane did not cry after all. She just sniffled and continued to put on her clothes.

"Is it true or it just seems to me that they have grown up? She would have burst out crying on the spot the other time. What's up with her? And she really seems to grow up, she looks taller. Well, thus, you won't even notice how you grow old, darling. You look at them every day, as you are their mother, and you don't even notice such things. It is amazing." She thought to herself.

"Ok, girls, if you need my help, you just tell me. I am going to wake up our men and check on the breakfast."

Kissing Jane on her forehead and patting Ailene's head she left the room, still amazed by the changes in her girls, especially by the fact that Ailene was almost of the same height as herself. "When has that all happened? I was not in a coma, was I? It's pretty strange."

The lamp was still on at the bedside in their bedroom, though the first merry sunbeams were trying to get through the thick curtains already. Diana came up to the window, pulled the curtains open, and could not resist from letting the morning air into the stuffy from the night sleep room. The fresh spring morning air gusted in filling the room with the mixed whiff of fresh grass, burnt leaves (obviously people started cleaning the parks from the last-year's dry leaves), and something else, very subtle, but very familiar… She was enjoying the calmness and beauty of that morning. There were few cars in the street, so she could hear the singing of birds and seldom barks of strayed dogs. She was distracted by the indistinct murmur behind her back. What Diana saw when she turned, made her smile widely. Her husband buried himself under their king-size duvet trying to stay warm, while her son, who evidently joined them at night, was snuggling like a baby wolf upon the duvet.

"And I need to wake these two Sleepy Sleepersons too. Why do they like to sleep that much? Ok, I'll give them another ten minutes." she thought looking at the wheezing couple. Inhaling deeply the fresh air she closed the window and went to check her girls again. "Omelet! Almost forgot!" she ran to the kitchen, switched off the stove, and returned to the girls' room. They had fully dressed already, and now each was combing their hair. Ailene's were like her mother's when she was a girl – long and thick, almost black with some tint of brown-gold at the edges, which were burnt out in the last summer sun. It was an utter ordeal to comb such hair back in the times when Diana was growing up. They had no conditioners or untanglers to treat her rebel hair. And now, when she looked at Ailene, who was calmly combing one side and then taking the brush by the other hand, patiently combing the other side, she was just happy that progress was so useful in her particular case, as the only thought of her daily morning fights with her own hair made Diana shrug. She cut hers as soon as she was out of school and was wearing short haircuts all her life after that.

Jane's hair was different. It was ash-brown, light, thin, and curly. At the age of three, or maybe closer to four, she probably realized that she was beautiful, as Diana noticed once that her little girl was looking at herself in the mirror as if looking for some flaws. Then she brushed her hair with her little fingers in one brisk move, shook her head, and started singing some kind of self-assuring song: "I am sooo beautiful! I am sooo beautifuuul! I have beautifuuul hair! La-la-la…"

"And why dad and Miras aren't getting up? Aren't they going anywhere? Why are we always the first to get up?" Jane couldn't stop whining still combing her curls. Diana knew that it was just her morning mood, as she was still sleepy. In the afternoon, when they both get back home from school, she will be flicking and singing, telling what happened at school non-stop. "How many hearts will this girl break? I hope she won't break them all and will keep a big one for herself…" these thoughts devoured Diana and the witty girl noticed that.

"Ma, you are not listening, aren't you? Aren't they going anywhere?" she repeated her question persistently.

"Yes, darling, yes. They are going. And I am going to wake them up. And you go have breakfast. Ailene, you are in charge. Everything is on the…"

"Yes, yes, yes, everything is on the table. Omelet on the stove, I'll put it on the plates, and will feed Jane." Ailene interrupted her quickly making herself sound like mom.

"How do you know we are having an omelet?" asked her sister.

"Can't you smell it? I smelt it when we were waking up, and kinda hoped that it would burn so that we won't eat it. Unfortunately, mom saved it just in time. Well, we'll have to eat those healthy whites…"

"And I like an omelet. And cereals, and I can even eat porridge." boasted Jane.

"Yeah, you can eat anything. And I hate porridges, and hardly bear the omelet. Thank God mom doesn't cook it very often. As she says, she varies with breakfasts." grumbled her older sister.

Their mother was standing at the door, listening to this morning discussion, and smiling at her daughters' arguments, until Ailene turned and flipped to her frowning: "And why are you standing here? What are you waiting for? Go and wake our dad!"

Diana jumped on the spot as she wasn't expecting that:

"Now she is using My words against me! Well, thank you, here they are, my grown-up girls!"

She dashed into the bedroom, sat on the bed, and started caressing her husband, rushing her fingers through his hair.

"Ok, daddy, now it's your turn to get up. Your daughters are going to fight for justice, they are full of resentment! They want you to get up immediately." she said pecking him on the cheek, and making sure that he opened his eyes, then she passed to the other side of the bed to wake up her son.

"Miras sweetie, come on, honey-bunny, wake up and sing. Let's go to the kindergarten. We'll get up, then wash up, then we will eat, and dress up. Then we will be ready to go, right?"

"Mhhm…" was the only sound that she could hear. It was not a two-year-old baby anymore, she could see a little man, trying to be like his father.

"Come on, sonny, wake up! Enough of sleep, come on." Diana was trying to sound strict, but her voice betrayed her. She could never be very strict with her beloved son.

When she finished with the girls' breakfast and having seen them off, Diana settled to have her morning tea, while her son was digging his portion of omelet with his fork.

"Let me help you, honey," she said to her beloved little son.

"No, I can do it," mumbled Miras with his mouth full. He just managed to put a piece of omelet into his mouth without dropping a crumb and was smiling at his success.

He did not like chitchatting much as his sisters did. Probably it was their never-ending talking that made him not so talkative. Or maybe it was his way of being like his father.

At this moment Dias came into the kitchen, just out of the shower, in his gown and slippers on his bare feet.

"O, omelet… And tea at once," he said sitting on his place at the table.

"How did you sleep?" asked him Diana not looking into his eyes.

"Ok," he said and started eating his breakfast.

"We did not even talk yesterday, as you came so late. And went to bed at once. Is everything ok at work?" she asked, trying to sound as casual as possible.

"A-ha, it's ok. By the way, today I am going to be late too. Our colleagues are coming from another city. We are going to arrange them evening leisure."

"Can anyone else arrange that leisure? Say, someone without family and obligations?"

"No, and they won't understand if I don't come. You better not think about it. And if you need me, just call, ok?" He said drinking his tea and getting up from the table. "And don't wait up, put kids to bed yourself."

"Ok, as usual, I know, it's not the first time. Just text me, you know me, I would be worried if you don't, and I wouldn't sleep anyway." she closed her eyes and shrugged. She could still remember the night when he was attacked near their house. He came home bleeding, but he was lucky to get away and remain safe with only six stitches on his head.

For a minute she was silent remembering again all details of that night, then she raised her head sounding very agile:

"So, are we all set? Not hungry anymore? Are we ready to go?"

"Yeah! Let's go to my kindergarten! Mom, can I watch a cartoon when I come home?" asked Miras jumping to the corridor.

"Of course, you can. In the evening you will watch. Let's go now. Or maybe we'll walk today? What do you say? The weather is just wonderful! It's so warm! Soon, very soon summer will come!"

While they were walking all her thoughts were with her husband. "What is going on with him? Another depression? Or middle-age crisis? Or something else? Or probably he has got someone, and now he is with that someone doing indecent things? Of course, not. He is at work right now, but in the evenings? Gosh, why on earth do men have such thing as a crisis? Why can't I let myself be in such a crisis once in a while? – That's it! I am bored! I want changes! I am sick and tired of taking care of children, of thinking about what to cook for breakfast, lunch, and dinner… I want to be free and young, huh? What do you say to that?" For a moment a flash of wildfire appeared in her eyes, which made her look young again, but just for a bit of a second. A tint of a smile touched her lips and disappeared in the corners of her passionate mouth.

"Ok, I got married when? Was I 22? Right. What have I seen? Of course, I saw things, but I had only one man… So, that's it? For the rest of my life? And I am sure that he had not one woman, but at least several. And at least three times – during my pregnancies and after labors. He should have someone, as I don't believe he was celibate for half a year every time I was in that condition. I was not attractive enough for him with my big tummy, though I was dying for sex myself. Those damn hormones! And I lived through that, look at me. What if I gave rein to my passions just for once? Though I cannot even imagine that I could do that… cheat on my husband."

With these thoughts, they approached the kindergarten. Diana led her son into his group, kissed him goodbye, and watched him run to his friends and toys, and join the common merry hum in the room without even turning to watch his mom leaving the room. Well, kids grow, and the more they grow the less they need parents….

"Damn, I have so many things to do, and I am car-less. I'll have to run back to the parking lot to get it. Should I get home or not? Ok, I'll get in later at lunchtime. Will be cooking dinner and cleaning up." thus clarifying the agenda for her day, Diana trotted back to her house.

At this moment her mobile phone rang. It showed that it was her close friend Janet. They knew each other since they were 8 years old but had no time to meet and talk lately.

"Hello, dear! How are you? Where are you? Me? Oh, I am all in errands, running here and there, busy as a bee. What about you? How are your boys? Do you want to talk? Ok, let's meet up today. But I need to see this specialist at nine. I made this appointment a really long time ago. I need to see this doctor badly; my neck makes me crazy. You know that it hurts me so long, and whatever I do, nothing gives results. Then I need to get my car to the service station, Dias made this appointment with his electrician. Maybe we will meet somewhere during lunchtime? No? Oh, you are busy. Then maybe in the evening? Though that's also not possible. Dias said that he will be late again, and I can't leave the kids all by themselves. Wait. What am I talking about? Diana has grown up already, still can't accept this fact, she can babysit with them. Let's meet somewhere in the neutral territory then. Call me when you are free. My battery is really weak, it lasts only one day, sometimes even less. So, I'll wait for a call from you somewhere closer to 7, ok? Ok, sweetie, kiss you. Don't be upset. There are no such problems that cannot be solved. Yes. See you!"

Diana was near the car when she finished talking. She looked at Susie, as she called her trusted friend – her car, checking it from outside, and quite satisfied she beeped it and opened the door. It was still cool from the nightstand in the street, so she sat on her front seat and started the engine to warm it up.

When she arrived at the clinic before the appointed time, she saw a crowd in the corridor in front of the doctor's door. "Ok, he must be a very good specialist, if so many people want to get to him…"

"Good morning, ain't the appointments run on a time basis? I signed for this appointment really long ago, and don't know if the situation changed since then…"

"Yes, yes, according to your time. And these ones here want to get to the doctor without appointments. They just mess around and don't let the good man work. You should have thought about making appointments beforehand, as we did." one of the "patients" was grumbling loudly in a squeaky and very unpleasant voice.

"Maybe they just found out that he is in town. By the way, any feedbacks? Has anyone come out yet?" Diana asked the same angry woman, who was still bragging about the invasion of the unwelcome people without appointments.

"Yes, one woman just came out so happy and pleased! Don't know what he was doing to her there, but her eyes were so shiny as if he was not doing her spine there… hmmm, but something else, if you know what I mean." she quacked with excitement and expectation a little bit gasping. "They say the doctor is young, handsome, and single… I am just wondering how he managed to become so skillful in his young age?" his future patient uttered suspiciously. Then she pierced Diana with her small sharp eyes and asked: "And what have you lost here? You don't look like you have any problems."

"Well, I have a problem and I am going to share it with the doctor himself. And I have a suggestion," she said it louder, so that everybody could hear her. "In order not to make a messy crowd here, let's put one unsigned person between the signed ones, and thus we will get to the doctor quicker, what do you say to that?"

"Let's do that!!!" the crowd supported her proposal cheerfully.

"I am not going to spend my time waiting for anyone getting in and out of the doctor's room!" the same woman was almost screaming in a high-pitched voice.

"Hey missy, are you in a hurry?" an elderly man approximately of her age addressed her smilingly. "We are not in the age to be in a hurry, right? And they are young," showing in the direction of the crowd, and then added: "they are always running somewhere. And we have nowhere to run, haven't we?"

Suddenly the old lady started smiling, and her face became absolutely kind:

"Well, where am I running? Nowhere. And it's better to talk to good people here. Right?"

Making a deep sigh not without satisfaction, Diana was then waiting for her turn to get in. She was just looking at the people coming and going when someone told her: "It's your turn now".

She knocked on the door and opened it:

"May I? Hello!"

If it was a movie, the operator would have probably chosen this angle and moment, slowing the frame shooting in order to show what impression our doctor made on Diana. Young, but not a boy, handsome, but not "magazine cover" handsome (she never liked those... too sweet), a bit harsh, his unshaved beard made him look macho-harsh, though unlike unshaved geologists or IT specialists. One could see that he could take care of himself, his hair was recently cut and very tidy. He was sitting and writing, obviously making last notes on the previous patient. She couldn't see his eyes yet, but she could imagine what they were like, probably very deep, and she was ready to dive into them. While she still couldn't see his eyes, her eyes were indulging the view of the doctor's gown covering the best body she had ever seen in her life. "This cannot be true! There are no such doctors! AAAhh! How on earth will I be treated by such a Man? Just looking at him makes my heart skip a beat, what if he touches me? And he will; he is a chiropractor! Ok, calm down, dear! Breathe in, breathe out! Breathe in, breathe... better? I think I am getting used to him. I wish he would have one of those squeaky voices, then the whole macho-image will be gone from my head, and I would be able to communicate with him decently..." However....

"How can I help you? I am listening carefully." the macho doctor said in a voice that made Diana's knees shake. She was lucky to seat herself on the chair before that and was waiting for the last surprise – meeting his eyes.

Putting his pen on the desk he raised his eyes at her and smiled. "Oh, and his teeth are just miraculous! Where on earth was he produced? And his eyes? I could follow him to the edge of the world just for those eyes. Someone must be lucky!" she said thinking that she was sitting in front of him like a rabbit in front of a boa, smitten and dazzled.

"I, errm.... Have a problem with my neck. It hurts. Here. For a long time already."

"All right, let me see."

He asked her to take off her blouse and stand up with her back to him. He stepped back to have a better look and wrote something down in his notebook. Then he came up to her and started palpating her neck: "Please tell if it hurts somewhere."

"Ok."

"What is your name?"

"Diana."

"Ok. Does it hurt here? Your muscles are so tense here. Tell me when and how you damaged your neck. You can put on your blouse, by the way. Now, please be seated and we'll write everything down. So, name is Diana. Surname?"

"Iskendirova."

"Year of birth?"

"1976."

"Good." he was repeating her answers and writing them down as she was answering. Diana thought he looked really cute, even imagined him as a diligent student at the moment.

"Have you had any fractures? No? Excellent."

"Any car accidents?"

"No."

"Wonderful. So, what happened to your neck?"

"Well, it happened during my first yoga class. The instructor did not warn that some asanas must be done carefully."

"Right. During yoga? Interesting. What did you do? Which asana was it? I am practicing myself, just trying to think of any traumatic situation. How could you damage your muscle?"

"Oh, God, he is killing me. He is practicing yoga? Tell me he is kidding. He cannot be that ideal!" and she replied out loud:

"It was a Plough asana. That was my first yoga class ever. And I am not flexible at all. And that was when the teacher tied me in such a knot that I felt nauseous at once, had a terrible headache. Then the coach said that if I felt all these symptoms then I shouldn't have done the asana at all. How could I know that? And the neck started to ache later. Not constantly at first. And now it is almost permanent, especially after my third labours." she said that blushing.

"Well, and you have kids. Even three of them…"

"Yes, two girls and a boy. Though why would I tell you that? Hmm…" replying to him, she continued that dialogue with herself.

"What are you doing, dear mother? Are you expecting anything… from this boy? He is your doctor and that's all. You will come to appointments; he will treat you and that is all. Out of sight, out of mind! You are crazy… Maybe he is gay!? Exactly! He is gay! It will be easier if you think that he is gay! Now, calm down. Breathe…"

And having concluded that the doctor was definitely gay, she was still devouring him with her eyes; while he was writing something in his notes without any suspicion of such emotional storm inside his patient's head, and the fact that he was thrown out of her "heterosexual men list".

"Here, I wrote my recommendations. I have got your information here. Try to avoid lifting heavy things, and that includes kids. What age are your kids? Are they grownups?

"Well, my youngest one is six now, going to be seven in winter." Diana replied and again continued saying to herself: "Why do you always give details? Just answer: Yes or No! Stupid! He's gay!!!"

The doctor went on:

"In that case, just don't lift heavy things. And you can come to appointments where I will start treating your neck properly next week. This will be your schedule, and here is my phone number in case you need any help… consultation, I mean, all right?" And he handed her a piece of paper with the handwritten recommendation of treatment.

"Oh, even his handwriting is not like a usual doctor's! So neat… Mmm… Stop it!"

"Thank you, doctor! Goodbye!" She said out loud to him and opened the door to leave.

"See you next week."

She went out of his office feeling like a schoolgirl, who got an A mark for her exam. She was blushing; her heart was racing like a rabbit's heart. She felt so elated that she didn't feel the ground and did not notice people in the queue around.

"Look, another one, with the same expression on her face!" She was returned to the ground by the unpleasant voice of the same elderly woman in the queue. "What did he say? Will he help?"

"Uh-huh..." mumbled Diana and raced out in the street full of different noises.

"Dear Lord, this is it! This feeling! That's what I was missing all these years! And nothing else matters. Look, how wonderful it is in the street! Birds are singing, the sun is shining! What is going on with me? Am I in love? Wow! Didn't know that love at first sight exists! Thank you, God, for creating such beautiful creatures for us to feast our eyes on them".

Dialing Deena's number, her other close friend from her first University, she was still hesitating if she should tell her about him. As she heard the long beeps, she decided that she will share and ask for advice.

"Hi darling, how are you? What are you doing? At home? Am I interfering with anything? No?" Not even giving her friend a chance to reply, she was asking all these usual questions one by one, so that she could get to the most interesting part quicker. "Well, ok. Listen, you are not going to believe this. What I just saw! I mean whom I just saw! A man! He's just a dream man! Handsome, muscled body, and hands... Ooohhh, his hands! And eyes! What? Where have I seen him? Oh, I went to my appointment with the chiropractor. He is a chiropractor. Doctor! He's just a prince from my fairy tales. What? Act? What do you mean? Oh, come on, he's a dream... This doesn't happen in reality. And he knows everything about my health problems and kids. And he said that I can come next week for the treatment. He gave me my appointment schedule for the next week and his phone number. Hmm... By the way, it's his mobile phone. Doesn't he have an office phone? Huh? You think he gave it on purpose? Oh, come on! Who needs an elderly woman with three kids if there are so many young and free girls around? Phew... I shared... Feels much better now! Now I am going to dream about him, silently. What else should I do? Call him? You are probably kidding! Noo, no way I am calling him. I will just go to the clinic on Monday and admire him again. Well, thank you for listening to me, my dear friend! Kiss and hugs to kids from me, ok?"

She realized that it was one of the most selfish conversations that she had ever had, but, luckily, Deena was one of the friends, who would understand and support if necessary, and the one, who would never accuse of being selfish or anything like that.

Without paying attention to anybody around Diana got back into her car and looked critically in the rear-view mirror. She noted that years indeed took advantage of her; there was no shine in her eyes anymore, subtle wrinkles around them. She patted her hair, sadly smiled, but as she remembered the young doctor, her eyes became so dreamy. With a sigh, she took the paper with the doctor's phone out of her pocket, where she put it while talking to Deena, looked at it again, and put it back into her purse.

"So, what now? Car service… What was the name of the electrician guy? Where did I write down his name? Oh, Dias texted me, I think. Ok, here it is. Rafael. Wow, what a name! I wonder if it is another God-created man… My brain won't be able to accept another handsome… Well, too old to dream about that honey, too old. Huh?" and with the scornful smile on her face, she started the engine and headed to the indicated address.

Having arrived at the place she found a queue of cars near the service station. "Another queue! This Rafael must be a good master too if so many people want to get to him". She switched on music in her car, opened windows, and started singing and humming together with her favourite singers while she waited for her turn.

Sun was warming up the spring air, birds were singing cheerfully. Diana could hear all this chirping above the sounds of the passing cars. Using her left palm as a shield from the sun to cover her eyes, she looked at two sparrows that were trying to get hold of a piece of a bun, which they found at the nearest playground. Each of them was pulling the bread on its side; at the same time, none of them realized that the piece was so big for both of them that they could easily share it and that would make both of them full at once. But the nature of any living being is to get something first, just in order to show the rest that you are quicker and stronger; and it is absolutely another question if you need that thing at all. They were so much overwhelmed with their fight that they did not notice a big pigeon that was sitting nearby, patiently watching the entertaining fight. It was coming closer and closer to the place of the quarrel and having caught the moment when these two were so engaged, with the last big leap the big guy just approached the sweet roll and having caught it with its beak flew away with its prey from the combative and foolish sparrows. They haven't even noticed at once that the bread was gone. And when they realized the loss, they started fighting even more fiercely, chirping very loudly. Then they noticed the big thief with their bun in its beak. Trotting around each other, still chirping and quite anxious, they looked as if they were weighing their chances to win. Evidently, their chances were low, so they decided to leave it and each of them flew away in different directions. "Ok, at least they are not revengeful," thought Diana, "otherwise they would fight to the end… just like people do".

Being so engaged by that sight she hardly noticed a man that came up to her open window.

"Ehem, excuse me, got a light?" he asked as Diana jerked as she heard his harsh voice so close to her.

"Oh, I haven't noticed you, I am sorry. Kinda scared me," she said that trying to smile. "What do you want? Smoke? Oh, sorry, I am not smoking."

"Ok, sorry for scaring you. Didn't mean to." the man said looking straight into her eyes, and then walked further to the next car in the line.

She waited for about an hour when it was her turn to get into the garage of the electrician. It was not a young man, very serious and very involved in whatever he was doing. Diana thought that he might even not look into people's faces and recognized them by the types of their cars. That number of cars waiting to be served by him did not give him a chance to relax from the early morning, but he seemed to enjoy his work.

"What's wrong with yours?" he asked sharply, imagining in his mind what her problem might be and how long it would take him to solve it. If it was a quick one, he might have a little break for a smoke outside.

"Well, there is something wrong with my alarm. It started several days ago. At first, there was something like a malfunction. I was driving and when I was approaching the crossroad my side blinkers started to blink together, so that another driver was signaling me, trying to say: "Hey crazy lady, choose one turn – left or right, and go there". Then during one heavy rain the other day I opened the car, got inside and the alarm went off. I could not switch it off or do anything about it. And now it does not work at all. You can kick the car or even steal it… it will not even squeak a bit."

"Ok, I see. I will check it. And you can wait over there." he said with relief. Not much to do, he was lucky to anticipate a smoke after that.

"Ok," Diana said getting out of the car. "How long will it take?"

"Just a sec, let me see," Rafael grunted trying to squeeze himself somewhere under the steering wheel. He lighted the spot with the flashlight in one hand, then reached something in the depth, pulled the wires to the light, and showed the problem place. It was a blown-up fuse.

"Half an hour tops. I will have to find a similar one and then change it," he said with relief. He was tired though it was still morning.

"Wonderful, and how much will it be?" Diana asked cautiously.

"For you 2000 Tenge. As I know your husband," he said winking at her, at the same time looking for the fuse on his shelves.

In thirty minutes, Diana was leaving the service station, quite pleased with the smooth flow of all the things that she planned to do.

"Ok, everything goes strictly according to the designated plan, boss," she recalled the famous phrase from the old Soviet movie that she liked. "Now, groceries and home. Will need to clean the house and then cook dinner. Ironing will wait till tomorrow". Thus, defining her further actions she headed for the closest supermarket.

Having bought all the things on the list that she had in mind and even more, she was pushing the loaded cart to her car with a lot of effort.

"How on earth am I going to drag this all home from the car? Oh, will have to go several times. Why do we still have no online shopping and delivery services like in Europe? You sit at home, order online and they bring it to you when it is convenient for you. God, how far we are from them! Ok, stop grumbling, old bag. We'll have it too, one day…" She got into her car and went home using the shortcut she was always using while going shopping.

She parked her car at her usual spot under the windows of her bedroom, though there was a place near the arch leading to the yard of their apartment house and that might be more convenient for her now. But Diana knew that in the morning this spot will definitely be blocked by other cars till nine – nine-thirty, and she needed to be early tomorrow, as she was going to her second daughter's concert at school and would not have time to wait for those cars to dissolve. She opened the back door and selected several pretty heavy plastic bags with meat and frozen food as she wanted to put them into the fridge first. Closing the door and bleeping the alarm on her keys, she slowly headed for the arch. At the entrance to the backside of the house, which was also a cooler and shady side of the house, she ran into her neighbor Rosa from the seventh floor. Asking each other usual polite questions about families and relatives, they were about to go each their own ways, when Rosa almost screamed:

"By the way, have you heard about the burglary? Yesterday, in our house, at the next entrance an apartment was ransacked. They took out everything. Can you imagine?! In the daylight! If there were our concierges, everything would have been all right, right? When they were sitting in our hallways, was it bad? Has anyone been robbed then? No! Who voted against them, huh?" panting with resentment Rosa was almost crying.

"Not me, definitely. And I am really sorry about the neighbors." Diana uttered completely busy with her thoughts. "Are the neighbors all right? They weren't at home at that moment, were they?"

"No, they were not. The woman with her child left for some errands in town. She says she has been postponing some bank payments and shopping and exactly yesterday she decided to do all the things on her "to-do list" and has not been home almost all day long. Usually, she sits at home with her baby, just like us." Rosa almost whispered. "Now I don't even know was she lucky or not!"

"Of course, she is lucky! Just imagine what it would be if they stayed home. Nowadays, ordinary people can kill each other, and a burglar can do it for his gain… All right, I have to go, my bags are really heavy, and I need to make another run for the rest of the bags." this last phrase she pronounced with effort as at that moment she was struggling with the bags trying to change them from one hand to another, as the fingers on her left hand became purple.

"Ok, I am gone too. See you." Rosa turned away already unzipping her sports jacket and ran away on her errands.

Well, neighbours are always a big issue. On one hand, you can keep in touch with them, sharing and participating in all the neighbourhood activities. On the other hand, you can just live without knowing many of them, as Diana did. So, when she met Rosa they talked about their families and relatives, were sympathetic about the misfortune that fell on their other neighbours, but the next moment, they were each busy with their own problems hardly ever remembering in the evening what they talked about in the morning.

Approaching her porch, she was annoyed by the thought that she will be having a major problem with opening the door with the pin code and then another door to her apartment with her hands loaded with heavy bags. She did not want to put bags on the ground as it was still wet and dirty after all the rains and dust brought by the crazy Astana winds from nearby buildings under construction.

She was about to make one bag slip to her wrist so that she could use that hand for entering the code to the door when someone caught that bag from behind and took it from her.

"May I? I see that you are having trouble here. Let me help you carry your bags to your door." suggested a stranger with a slight accent.

"Hi, where did you come from? Who are you? I haven't even noticed you approaching me." her hand stopped halfway to the door, but both her hands were shaking already as she was exhausted holding the bags for so long. She jerked her hand with the bag not giving it to the stranger. "What's wrong today with everybody? Can I get home today or not? And who the hell is he at all? Maybe he is that burglar… polite, but still a burglar?" She said it to herself.

"Oh, I know what you are thinking!" her thoughts were interrupted by the same cheerful voice of this Caucasian man[3], who was still trying

---

[3] Caucasian man – a man from Caucasus, Russian Federation (there are several nations living there – Chechen, Balkar, Kabardin,etc.)

to take the bags from Diana's hands showing with all his appearance that he wanted only to help.

"Well, and what am I thinking about? Only tell it quicker, as I am really tired of holding these bags." Diana uttered panting.

"Well, who is he? Why should I believe him? Huh? And with this burglary in the house... Very suspicious... Something like that?" He said smiling. It was an ordinary Caucasian man in his middle forties, with receding hair and very lively eyes. "My name is Arthur. I am your new neighbor. I live on the fourth floor, a 1-room apartment in the middle. I moved in just recently, that's why you haven't seen me before. Let go of these bags, please, your fingers are really scary purple already."

"Ok, Diana. My name is Diana. Sorry, can't shake your hand now." she smiled, and her smile lingered on her lips. The name of her new neighbor reminded her of one comic show character. "Arthur Pirozhkov, I think. Yes, there was even a song about him! Arthur Pirozhkov will make your husband a cuckold! Exactly! Used to be very popular." Though there was a big difference in appearance. The TV Arthur was a muscled hairy macho, and Arthur the neighbor was distinguished with compactness – his height and the body was less than an ordinary man's.

She almost laughed out loud as she remembered the song and the whole image of the other Arthur while the real Arthur already took the bags from her, entered his own pin, and opened the door.

"Well, I am very pleased, really!" Diana said entering the elevator and pressing the button of her floor. "What is your floor? You said fourth? Ok. I live on the second. Now, you can come and ask for any help you need. Don't be shy. Ok?" As she said that the elevator stopped at her level.

There were two bicycles on the floor near her apartment door, one pink with purple tassels and one smaller with supportive wheels of dark blue colour.

"Wow, according to this," looking at the little "car park" started Arthur, "I may assume that you have two children – a girl and a boy."

"Actually, there are three of them. The oldest one prefers roller skates." Diana clarified.

"I wouldn't even think that you have children. And three... Wow." the neighbor smiled.

"So, you thought that all this food is just for me?" Diana laughed with slight indignation. "So you say! Ok, thank you very much for your help! Sorry, cannot invite you in for a cup of tea or coffee. There is such a mess at home as if an army marched through the place. I'll be digging out those piles now. Three kids are not one. They bring demolition three times more."

"Oh, you don't say so! Children are wonderful! I love kids!" Arthur unwillingly returned to the elevator smiling and waving to Diana goodbye.

"Ok, thanks again, Arthur. You can come down to us in the evening; I will introduce you to my husband. Maybe you will become friends with him and will watch football together now and then." suggested Diana opening the door with her key.

The doors of the elevator opened, and Arthur entered it saying again: "Ok, thanks! Bye. It was nice to meet you…", and obviously something else, but she could not hear it, only the sound of a moving elevator.

Diana sighed as she entered her apartment, smiling at the thought that it was a rare day rich with communication with men. "Well, at least some sort of distraction for me! Dias is always at work or on business trips. In the evenings he is tired, just watches TV, then eats and then TV again. We never get the chance even to talk. And I had two men to talk to today! What a day!" She remembered her wonderful doctor and suddenly became sad.

"Why haven't I met him earlier… some twenty years ago?" she kept thinking finally putting the bags on the floor in the corridor.

"Uh-huh, he was probably just born then," Diana answered to herself. "Ok, even so, what would you do with him now? Huh? That's it! Dreams are dreams… Enough of dreams! You must be cleeeaning the house! Look at this bedlam here!"

"Ok, cleaning it is then! What about the rest of the bags? I need to bring them too. Well, I'll clean up first and then will fetch them. There is nothing melting or spoiling in those bags – some pasta, powders, soap, and juices. They can wait." Thus, talking to herself Diana brought those bags to the kitchen and started sorting out the meat and placing it in the freezer, leaving one piece for today's dinner.

She was busy talking to herself, which was a usual thing for our Diana, taking out all the meat from those bags to the big table. When she turned around to take a knife and a cutting board from the desk near the sink, she thought she saw someone sitting on the bed in her bedroom. Their apartment was of a square form, quite symmetrical, leaving the corridor in the middle. And one could see what was going on in the bedroom from the kitchen and from the living room one could see a part of the children's room. As Diana was absolutely sure that she was home alone and it only seemed to her that she saw something, she decided to finish with the meat first and then go and check the room and start to put the scattered around things that they all left as they were leaving in the morning back in their places. "Apparently Miras left one of his big toys on our bed. And if it is that huge panda, I will have to shake our bed cover out! What kind of a toy is that!? Its wool or hair falls off like during the molting period of real pandas! And I am not even sure if real pandas have that molting thing." saying this to herself she put different pieces of meat in different plastic bags separating them into "first" and "second" courses, pieces with bones were going for soups and the filets were going to be "stewed meat", "casserole" and other tasty things that she was often "spoiling" her family with. Leaving one big piece of filet on the table she prepared an onion, a carrot, and eight big potatoes for cooking the casserole for dinner. But looking at the clock on the wall she realized that it was still too early for cooking dinner – meat would be ready in an hour and a half, plus half an hour for all the veggies. "Dias usually comes home at half-past seven, and today he is going to be late, so no need to hurry with dinner at all, and it's only 2:15 pm. Girls will be back from school around 4 pm, so I've got some time for the housework". It was lunchtime but Diana was not hungry, so she decided to drink a glass of water and start that cleaning after all.

Having finished with the meat, she washed her hands, wiped them with the kitchen towel, and went out to the corridor to define the scope of work as they say. She remembered that she was going to check the bedroom and see if her suspicions about the panda were true at all. She made one step in the direction of the room when a big, strange man in his boots on went out of her bedroom looking straight into her eyes.

* * *

Most people behave similarly when they are frightened or under stress. They start to scream, cry or they run away, trying to escape the danger by any means. Diana was different for sure. Since her young age, she never screamed or cried out loud for help as any other girl would do. She could cry but she never screamed or squeaked, could never do that. Probably, instinctively she understood that in the moments of danger squeaking or running away or panic would not really help. This inability to scream somehow influenced the development of her life. Once in winter, when she was probably in grade six of secondary school and fourth in her music school, she was going to her solfeggio class. It was some time in the morning; the snow was everywhere covering all the ground, trees, and buildings, no wind as she could hear the crunchy sound of her boots on the snow. There were people in the streets going here and there, and it was quite peaceful, and nothing seemed to forebode the bad. Her road was going through her ordinary school where she knew all the corners, and she didn't even notice a man standing at some distance from her in the backyard of her school. What was she thinking about then? Maybe about a boy from another class, whom she fancied then? Or maybe she was thinking about her "beloved teacher" of solfeggio, who was always picking at her? She was then distracted from her thoughts by the sound of quickly approaching steps on the crispy snow. Diana thought that someone wanted to outrun her on that path and was not even scared when someone grabbed her from behind in a very tight hold and was obviously trying to throw her on the snow. "That man standing behind the school was probably some maniac waiting for his victim!" – The thought flashed through her mind. But the man did not take into consideration that his victim might be taller than himself, so he failed in his attempt to throw her on the ground. And visible calmness of the prey confused the maniac. Though inside Diana was screaming with horror and anticipation of what that man was going to do to her, and her thoughts were rushing away in different directions not leaving a chance to find any solution to help her escape. She opened her mouth, but the shriek did not come out. Instead, as her mouth was open already, she asked the man: "What do you want?" in a quite suppressed voice. Apparently, he was stunned by the question or the way she asked it, so somehow, he loosened the grip, and Diana caught the opportunity at once. She stepped aside looking calmly into his eyes and the only thing he had to do was to apologize and retreat from the scene of the 'uncommitted crime'. What was going on in the girl's heart at that moment? Well, she managed to walk to the music school and sit down on the bench inside the building near the wardrobe. And that's when she started to panic, she was all trembling, she could hardly breathe, her heart was about to jump out of her throat, she felt nauseous. Later, in the lesson she could hardly concentrate on the subject, and the teacher, definitely mad at 'such attitude to the subject' was giving her even more tasks than to the rest of the group.

She told about it to her friends at school, but somehow never shared it with her parents as she was ashamed.

The second case took place when she was nineteen. A son of her father's old school friend came to look for a job in town and stayed at their place, as it happened most of the time when some relative or "old friend" came to town, they always stopped at their kind uncle's. He was thirty-three years old, and by that time he was divorced already. Her hospitable parents offered him to stay at their house while he was looking for a job and a room in a hostel or apartment for rent. And the young man turned out to be "a snake in their bosom". He noticed the pretty and shy girl, who was just nubile as he thought, and she did not even know about that. She did not think of guys at that age, and about dates and kisses, though… No, she thought about all of that, but only thought, as she had no time to meet those guys in person. She studied at the University, was reading a lot, writing course papers, had internships at schools; in short, she was acting like any normal "bluestocking" would act. So, she was so busy that she did not even notice that this homely man with an unpleasant little moustache and shifty eyes paid attention to her. Once, her parents were invited to their neighbours, and Diana and Zhak stayed home. Diana was doing her homework and preparing for the next day's open lesson in the tenth grade, where students were quite advanced and were waiting for any single mistake from their new and young intern-teacher so that they could mock and laugh at her. Therefore, she was trying to make her lesson interesting and informative. She was always using hand-made wall-newspapers and any pictures that she could prepare herself, as those days there were no computers or any overhead projectors that teachers could easily use.

That day she was preparing one of her wall newspapers; when she was sharpening her pencil and at the same time taking a critical look at her "work", she cut her finger really badly. It started bleeding and she ran into her parents' bedroom as there was the place where they kept all medicines and a first-aid kit. In the room, she bent to her mom's bedside table to get the band aid or something, when someone grasped her from behind and threw her on the bed. She did not understand what it was and who it was, though she realized that there was only one man beside her in the house. She recognized the smell of his sickly-sweet cologne. She tried to release herself from his clinch and all she could do was that she just turned facing him.

"Get off of me." she hissed.

"Oh no, now you are not going to escape," he said contentedly pressing the girl into the bed and restraining her hands.

"It's not going to happen, moron," trying to smile, and not showing her fear, Diana spoke through her teeth again.

She was losing her strength trying to get rid of his grip; she wanted to reach for something essential from the bedside table that she could hit him with. In the meantime, he was relishing his position kissing her cheek, as she was turning away her face every time he tried to get her lips. Having found nothing useful on that table and throwing everything she touched on the floor – mom's powder box, compact mirror, a leaflet with the new movie ad from the local cinema… She was losing her frail hope of escaping the menacing act of violence. When suddenly someone opened the door of the bedroom and she saw her dad in his coat and hat, shocked and not believing his eyes, and definitely not expecting to see this in his bedroom. He threw the "rapist" on the floor and helped his daughter get up from the bed. She did not remember whether her dad hit Zhak in his face or maybe not, it did not matter. He saved her; this was all that really mattered. Diana did not cry, she was all shaking, breathing heavily, her cheeks were red, and her hair all messy because of the fight with the stronger rival, but she was very happy to be saved.

What really happened next, she did not want to recall and remember at all, as it was a real nightmare for her.

* * *

As usual, struggling with the panic attack, but never showing it off, Diana cleared her throat and suppressing the nervous chuckle, uttered:

"Eerm... You are probably lost? Wrong apartment?" trying to turn everything into a joke. "Oh, you are like that man from that old Soviet comedy! What was his name? Zhenia Lukashin? Lukashov? You got into a wrong house or... city?" she talked and talked while in her head there was a whole process of site evaluation: "What is that man? Who is he? What does he want? He doesn't look like a drug taker, doesn't look like a drunk (don't feel the smell of alcohol) ... Looks shabby, unshaved, but not that long ago. His shirt is tatty, not ironed, the jacket is baggy, either it was not his originally, or this man lost a bunch of kilos. His eyes are definitely firm, and there is something frightening about them. What is on his mind? And his face looks familiar, maybe I have seen him somewhere... don't remember talking to him though. Or... he might be that home robber?"

"May I help you anyway? Are you lost?" Diana continued out loud without taking her eyes off her uninvited guest, her voice became tense. "Why are you silent? Do you need help?" she insisted.

"No, I don't need your help," the man's voice was dry and harsh. "I can deal with it myself."

"Huh, then you Can talk. Well, if you are a burglar, then you can take all the gold, all valuable things, money after all." Diana pierced this strange man that somehow got into her house with her wary eyes. "And when you are done, please leave, as I intend to clean the house before my kids arrive from school."

"Why would I need all of those things that I bought for you myself? She wants to clean the house, and manage to slip out to see her lover before her husband is at home, huh? Well, surprise, I am here! What are you staring at me like that? Say you don't recognize me? Only five years passed since that... You haven't changed obviously, well, only hair is different. I provided you with everything, I did everything for you. And you always thought it was not enough, right? Always looking at someone else. You left me, now you decide to cheat on him too?" he spitted it out in one breath, all red and excited; she could see the beads of sweat on his forehead.

"What are you talking about? You are definitely taking me for someone else!" Diana resented.

"Well-well, you better tell me where they help to clear your memory away that you forget your past? And I see that you updated your "random access memory". And I'm a dumb ass that still cannot do it… All these years I was only thinking of how I will track you down… and…" his nostrils suddenly became tense and wide, eyes fixed; and he finished the sentence through the gritted teeth. "And have my revenge. Do you want to know what I was doing during these five years? What happened to my business and me?"

"Do I have another choice?" the frightened woman uttered. She realised that this man was definitely not a burglar, but evidently, he was out of his mind, and he didn't even hear what she was asking about. All she had to do was to listen to him and do her best to avoid an aggressive attitude from the "stranger-husband".

"When you left to your lover boy, I could hardly rest at all!" He started shouting. "I could not understand what I have done wrong. Why did you decide to cheat on me, take my children and run away? All these thoughts, they were killing me, making me insane. I started drinking, but alcohol did not help neither to forget you nor live further on. This was a dead end. I started taking drugs, but they didn't help either. I lost interest in my business, and my people were abandoning me, some of them tried to help though, but none of them had the patience to look after me. I didn't turn up at work… Why would I? Anyway, I was drinking there and sleeping in my office. All days were alike. While I still had the money I tried different drugs, though I don't even know what they were. In that state that I was, that was the last thing that I was worried about. Those pills were having some effect on me of being stuck somewhere in between two worlds… endless labyrinths – so white that you could not even figure out where the floor or where the walls, doors, or passages were… Dark labyrinths were making me feel so hopeless. It was just like walking in the sheer darkness with your eyes wide open trying to notice anything that your eye would catch. Always bumping into some wall… Feeling your own short breath or maybe someone else's behind your back. Those were the moments when I wanted to wake up and reassure myself that it was just a nightmare, and you would soothe me. But the nightmare was endless. And I was always looking only for you and always failed. I was thinking about you all the time, even unconscious.

I did not even know before that I loved you so much after all those years of our married life. Do you remember how we lived? Weren't we happy? I was working; you were sitting at home with our kids. I was bringing everything you wanted. Yes, I travelled a lot, but it was part of my job. And yes, I had some affairs now and then, but those were just "overhead costs" you know. Was there anything missing from the list of orders that you sent to me every day? Was there? All those thoughts were driving me crazy! But I did not die, though I was hoping that one day I would drop off the hooks because of overdose or cirrhosis. You know my body; it is not like others'. I did not die, moreover, I did not lose my mind… and that's when I decided to find you… even though you said that you would leave the city. I started to look for your friends, but whenever I approached any of them, they were running away from me as if I was infected with a plague. Now I can imagine how scared they were to see me. Some of them did not even recognise me, some of them gave money for a bracer, but all of them wanted to pass by me as quickly as possible. None of them told me where you were. All of them were accusing me of what happened between us… But why me? Why was it my fault? It was You who left me!!!" he stopped to take a breath. His eyes were burning with mad fire, his mouth was distorted as he shouted the last phrase.

"Oh my God, so many things happened in this man's life. And he blames me! How should I prove to him that it was not me? Man, and it's not the first time when I am taken for someone else… and as it turns usually out, that someone is not a very good person… How "lucky" I am to get into such situations. I remember the first time when one girl almost attacked me accusing me of having affair with her boyfriend, also setting up some of her friends, and sleeping with some women's husbands, just a devil in a skirt! When I managed to prove to her that I am not Elvira we even managed to laugh together. Well, it was more fun those days…"- these thoughts ran through her head, she was almost smiling when she was reminded of the horrid reality she was in.

"You left me," he repeated drily. But the tone of his words was far from soothing, as the wrath in his eyes was boiling resembling the volcanic lava that was ready to disgorge.

"I need to do something with this nice man… otherwise, there will be victims…" Diana thought. She did not say anything out loud as she understood that any of her words could become that detonator that would make everything only worse. But she was also aware that her silence won't help her either. They were still standing at the entrance to her bedroom in the corridor. There was a table with the telephone base on it. Diana glimpsed at it and thought if she could manage to dial the police.

But her "jealous husband" caught that glimpse and hissed glaring at her:
"Don't even think about it!"

"I wasn't thinking about it. Though, to be honest, I had that thought. But the idea is bad itself… I wouldn't be able to dial it without you noticing it. And to explain to our police what is going on here… that is a separate story, one should need a lot of patience and time most of all. Ok, I give up. Shall we go to the kitchen, have a cup of tea, coffee, maybe get to know each other?" Diana suggested that, very surprised with her bravery or silliness, or was it despair?

"Tea?" He was confused by her reaction, but weighing all options, took her under her arm and dragged her to the kitchen. He seated himself at the table and said in expectation:

"Well, tea it is! As in good old times. Do you remember when we lived at the Mir avenue? Our house was one of the highest buildings then, later other bigger houses were built there. Our spacious apartment on the seventh floor, to the right from the elevator." there was something kind and warm in his eyes as he was recalling all that. However, a moment later they gained that dark ominous tint again promising nothing good to Diana.

"I thought you loved me. You met me every day, smiled at me, chattered about kids, went to bed with me… and were lying all the time.

Constantly and mercilessly. How many times did you cheat on me, huh? Did you love me at all? Did you?"

Diana was standing in her kitchen staring at that strange man trying to understand him. And this moment of his nostalgia for the relationship between a husband and a wife made her think about her own life with her husband, the relationship that was really worn out if to be honest with herself. If to think of it and compare, then they were approximately at the same place where this poor man found himself a long time ago absolutely sure that his marriage was stable and happy. What was she thinking then? Did she still love her husband after all those years of happiness and mishaps? She picked the kettle and went to the sink to pour the filtered water into it. While the water was filling the kettle, she looked at her "husband" and started to understand his wife. She was probably tired of waiting for the permanently exhausted "master of the house". Every method to revive their marriage was used; every new approach to enlighten their relationship was field-tested. And she probably was tired of being treated only as the mother of their children or a housewife with no other interests than her kids and family. And after all these years of desperate attempts to change this attitude, there were only two ways out for her: either she forgot about all her dreams and lived "for the sake of kids", as most people did; or she forgot about her eternally "strayed" husband, quitted waiting up for him with warm dinner and lived in full, and a lover was not an exception. All this was ok until one of them started considering a divorce. Obviously, his wife chose the second option. As for Diana herself, she was somewhere in the middle, suspended. Her husband and she herself were more friends rather than lovers. They met when they were getting their second degrees at the university. They were together almost twenty years for that moment, and they got used to each other so much that were tired of each other. Any business trip that Dias was on she took as a small vacation. They haven't called each other during the workday for the last ten-twelve years unless there was something really urgent in the family. No funny or sexy texts that they used to send to each other, nothing similar, since she had their first baby. They hadn't been out for a long time either, no cinemas, no cafes, just family friends or relatives where they were invited in "full set".

If at the very beginning when Dias was going out somewhere with his friends, Diana was saying to herself that she could not join him as their kids were too small. But time passed, kids were growing up, Dias's habit to spend evenings and nights with his "friends" remained the same, he never offered her to join him, and Diana's trust started to shake. As she was brought up in the atmosphere of mutual understanding, love, and trust, she never allowed any bad thoughts to get into her mind. She realised that he might have some affairs now and then that she chose not to think of; and that she could never allow to herself. Just to have sex with the first guy she met somewhere? The idea itself made her shrink with disgust. But she could fall in love with some man, who might be an ideal husband to her. And it was not a man himself, but just the image of someone else besides her husband. And these men usually did not even suspect of Diana's feelings to them. It could be any good-looking guy with a bright smile, athletic body, and lots of other dignities that he acquired thanks to Diana's rich imagination, as there were no such men in real life that she knew and that could have all those qualities. At that moment she recalled the doctor, who could easily replace all those made-up men in her head.

Yes, she could understand this "husband's" wife, she understood her so well and so clearly that words started to come out of her mouth themselves:

"Yes, I was sick and tired of waiting for you every day, sick of waiting and hoping that maybe today he would finally look at me as a woman, not just a housewife or a dishwasher. That you would realise that I am a woman, not just the mother of your children. That I also have some needs, wishes, or interests. But you hardly even noticed me. That is why at first, I gave up. First of all, it is very difficult to believe that after three labours you are still irresistible especially when no one cheers you up. Of course, I gained some weight and was wearing loose clothes. And those days when you were spending evenings at home, I was trying to draw your attention to me, even though I was tired of cleaning the house, taking care of kids. Still, I was buying some sexy nightgowns that were unbelievably uncomfortable and very open... I was waiting for you in our bedroom, and you did not even enter it as you were watching TV in the living room lying on the floor and falling asleep there later. Secondly, all your help to me was to take them to school or nursery, all the rest things – whether kids were sick or happy running in the street, I was always doing everything myself – daily and nightly. You cannot even imagine that sometimes I slept only a couple of hours a day and somehow remained sane. That is why when children grew up a little, I decided that it was time to pull myself back together. I stopped pitying myself and allowed myself to relax during the day sometimes, despite a pile of your shirts that needed to be ironed. I started to gain self-respect again. And I realised it when other men noticed me. Absolutely strange men were making compliments to me, while you were living your own life paying attention neither to me nor to the changes that I was going through. And now I enjoy it when other men look at me. I see that they like me, and I like that too. And you cannot even imagine what is going on in my head. That is why when I met one man, for whom I became really close to his heart, and not because of money or anything, but just because he forgets about anything in the world when I am near him, I couldn't resist. I tried to suppress my feelings, to find all the reasons to stay in my marriage thinking of children and the future. Tried to persuade myself that I must do it for the sake of children, be patient and understanding.

Do you know how many times I tried to draw your attention to me? Do you know how many times I was crying on my pillow even lying next to you in one bed and you didn't even hear me, or maybe you chose not to hear me at all. How many times was I making attempts to talk to you? All in vain! You were always busy, were always finding anything to keep yourself busy. So, my dear. This is a two-way street; one must take into consideration all the participants of the road traffic. And now you want to ask me why? You men always think that wives should just sit at home, raise your kids, never complain, and always support their husbands. But have you ever thought that you might feel just a little respect for what they do at home? That you may also take responsibility for the upbringing of your children... yes, our children, not only mine. So that when they grow up and "misbehave" as you would think, or not listen to what you say to them, then you won't accuse your wives of bringing up children badly... because you will be aware that you were there too to give your piece of wisdom or whatever a father should give to his children. And the fact that you were too busy spending evenings and nights with some other women or even your friends, won't make your children respect you, as they haven't seen you most of the time. You weren't there for them at nights when they cried, you weren't there to soothe their pain when they fell off their bicycles and you weren't there to explain that they may fall, but what more important in life is that they must always get up and move on.

"Ok, you want to say that I am a bad father?! I always gave money for anything you needed to buy for them. I was arranging trips to anywhere they wanted!"

"You don't even listen to me! I just told you that money is nothing if you can't spend a normal evening with your children playing, not sitting at your computer or TV shushing them away."

"But they must remember me! I was always bringing them any toys they wanted!"

"Yes, they remember their toys. There are loads of them. And a lot of other people (relatives and friends) bring them different toys as well. It doesn't matter who brought what... the main thing is the personal attitude. Remember my mom? She never brought anything huge or expensive and it was not because she didn't want to. It was because she knew that we could get them anything they liked. She could bring small toys for each of them or some dresses or even pyjamas, but they would remember and value that, because she was talking to them, telling stories, watching their favourite cartoons with them, laughing with them, going for a walk with them. And even if she is not with us anymore, they still remember and miss her.

"But I am their father! They must love me!" he roared.

The kettle switched off automatically and in the tense silence, this cry of a man sounded so desperately. He was standing at her back now and she was startled to see him so close now. Diana realised now that he wasn't the one to whom she should be telling those words, but she felt so good that she did. It was as if she found a clue to her own life. And she was thinking of talking to Dias in the evening definitely! If she hears his opinion, she will know what to do next! This thought made her smile with the new hope for the new stage of her life.

"Are you mocking me? Are you making fun of me?" Her smile made him furious.

"Uh-oh, wrong reaction... don't panic, everything should be alright..." She was looking straight into his eyes trying to tame her heart so that he could not hear it and thus feel her fear. But she failed... the beast felt the prey and was ready to pounce.

The next moment he seized her by her throat and was trying to strangle her with his strong grip.

"I can't die like that... This is ridiculous... I don't... Oh my kids... what if he takes them and runs away..." Diana was trying to unclench his hands off her neck... fighting for her life, but she was losing this battle. "Why do they say people see all their lives running through in front of their eyes before they die? Don't... see... any..thing.... like... that. What... will... be... with... kids...?"

It was hard to stay focused and conscious. Everything in her eyes became purple. She felt how the last oxygen molecules were absorbing in her blood. She could hear her heart beats so distinctly rare, uneven, and abrupt.

"This is it... I'm in God's hands now," and she loosened her hands hanging in the insane man's hands like a puppet.

Diana woke up all sweaty. Her heart was still rushing, her throat and mouth so dry that she couldn't even produce saliva to swallow it and somehow wet her mouth.

"Water! I need water! What the... I thought I was really dying. Phew... what a nightmare..."

She sat up in her bed and looked around. It was dawn. The electronic clock on her bedside table showed 6:02. It was the 27th of April on the calendar...

www.ingramcontent.com/pod-product-compliance
Lightning Source LLC
LaVergne TN
LVHW040200080526
838202LV00042B/3252